# THE HOLIDAY OF A MARQUESS

LINDARAE SANDE

Twisted Teacup
PUBLISHING

The Holiday of a Marquess



V1

Cover photograph © Period Images.com

Background cover image © DepositPhotos.com

Cover art by Twisted Teacup Publishing

All rights reserved - used with permission.



http://www.lindaraesande.com

ISBN: 978-1-946271-63-1

Twisted Teacup Publishing, Cody, Wyoming

# ALSO BY LINDARAE SANDE

*The Daughters of the Aristocracy*

The Kiss of a Viscount

The Grace of a Duke

The Seduction of an Earl

*The Sons of the Aristocracy*

Tuesday Nights

The Widowed Countess

My Fair Groom

*The Sisters of the Aristocracy*

The Story of a Baron

The Passion of a Marquess

The Desire of a Lady

*The Brothers of the Aristocracy*

The Love of a Rake

The Caress of a Commander

The Epiphany of an Explorer

*The Widows of the Aristocracy*

The Gossip of an Earl

The Enigma of a Widow

The Secrets of a Viscount

*The Widowers of the Aristocracy*

The Dream of a Duchess

The Vision of a Viscountess

The Conundrum of a Clerk

The Charity of a Viscount

***The Cousins of the Aristocracy***

The Promise of a Gentleman

The Pride of a Gentleman

***The Holidays of the Aristocracy***

The Christmas of a Countess

The Knot of a Knight

The Holiday of a Marquess

***The Heirs of the Aristocracy***

The Angel of an Astronomer

The Puzzle of a Bastard

The Choice of a Cavalier

The Bargain of a Baroness

The Jewel of an Earl's Heir

The Vixen of a Viscount

The Honor of an Heir

The Rose of a Sultan's Son

***The Ladies of the Aristocracy***

The Lady of a Grump

The Lady of a Sultan

The Wager of a Wallflower

***Beyond the Aristocracy***

The Pleasure of a Pirate

The Making of a Mistress

# CHAPTER 1
# A WIDOW'S THOUGHTS ON
# A CLUB

*D*ecember 21, 1816, Soho Club, London
Barely aware of the light snow that was falling beyond the dining room windows of the Soho Club, Elaine Mary Ludlow Denberg, Countess of Montaine, dipped a newly sharpened quill into an ink pot and began to write.

> *Dear Adeline,*
> *Your insistence that I remain in London for Christmas-tide did not fall on deaf ears. Your gift of the calling card has also been put to good use, as I write to you from the most elegant dining room of the Soho Club.*

Here, Elaine paused. Had anyone but Adeline Carlington, Marchioness of Morganfield, told her of the existence of the Soho Club, Elaine might not have believed them. From the few people she had seen since arriving the night before, carrying only a valise followed by a footman charged with her trunk, she had thought the exclusive club might be for women only. Even the person who seemed to be in charge of the club was a woman.

Mrs. Skarsgard had welcomed her with a warm smile, given a quick glance at the card she carried, and then asked, "Pink, blue, green or yellow?"

Not about to ask Mrs. Skarsgard what she meant—she'd had quite enough of answering queries that day—Elaine simply said, "Pink."

Handing her a key, Mrs. Skarsgard said, "It's quite private and preferred by our long-time female members. End of the hall, last door on the right." She had motioned with a hand in the general direction of the room before dipping a curtsy and returning to her desk.

Elaine remembered regarding the key as if it might explode. But a moment later, she was using it to unlock a door. When she opened that door, well, she tittered.

Pink, as it turned out, referred to the color of the room's decor. It was awash in pink. The silk-covered walls, the velvet drapes and counterpane, and even the Turkish carpet were all variations of the color pink.

She ignored the footman's curious expression as he placed her trunk atop a deep chest of drawers. He bowed and was about to take his leave when she remembered she should give him a coin.

"I cannot accept it, my lady, but I thank you for the consideration," the rather tall young man said when he saw she was attempting to open her reticule. He bowed again and shut the door behind him.

Her opinion of the Soho Club having risen yet another notch, Elaine turned and caught her reflection in a dressing table mirror near the window. The pink walls were obviously good for her complexion, for she looked younger than she felt. She was almost giddy now that she could be alone.

Amusement had been hard to come by that day, or any day for the past nine months. The death of a husband was probably hard on every woman. For her, it had been a combination of relief and grief, sadness and shock.

Now that her oldest son and the heir to the Montaine earldom, Graham, had finally taken up residence in the Montaine mansion in Park Lane—he'd had a bachelor quarters of his own in The Albany until the month prior—she thought it best she vacate the premises for a few days. He was nearly thirty years old, and although he hadn't yet taken a wife, Graham announced he was on the verge of courting. He had informed her with his next few words that he did not wish to hear any of her recommendations for eligible young females—not that she had any—nor did he intend to accompany her to any of the winter time entertainments.

As if she could attend them.

She was still in half-mourning, and she would probably continue to wear her lavender gowns for another few months. Still, the hurt she had felt at hearing her son's rebuke was still raw.

Reminded of the conversation that had her instructing her lady's maid to pack a trunk, Elaine struggled to hold back the tears. She took some solace in knowing her younger son, Gabriel, would never say such things. Besides, he looked forward to taking a wife, and she was sure he already had a viscount's daughter in mind for the position.

Elaine shook her head, determined to return her attention to the letter.

*I was quite surprised and rather pleased to discover my room is pink. As I am still wearing lavender every day, I have felt as if I have been surrounded by it these past few months; I find the pink a refreshing change. I admit to feeling as if I was a young girl when I climbed into bed last night. Oh, and*

*what a comfortable bed it is, with the softest of mattresses
and linens so fine, I felt as if I was a guest of the queen.*

Pausing to read what she had written, Elaine's thoughts
returned to the day before. To her first impressions of the
Soho Club. The incident with the footman wasn't the only
notable occurrence. There had been a maid who knocked on
her door as she was preparing for bed. A maid who carried a
tray upon which sat a steaming cup of chocolate.

"I'm very sorry to disturb you, my lady, but would you
like a cup of chocolate?"

Elaine remembered blinking. *Had she fallen asleep? Was it
already morning?* But the maid jerked her head in the direction of the office and said, "Mrs. Skarsgard thought you
might wish it after your day of travel."

Well, bless Mrs. Skarsgard. Elaine had only traveled
from Park Lane, but it had been a trying day. "Do give her
my thanks," Elaine said as she took the cup from the tray.
"And thank you, as well."

She remembered holding the cup between her hands,
allowing the warmth to penetrate her cold fingers before she
drank it in only a few gulps.

After that, sleep had come easily. Waking earlier than
usual, she had thought first to do her correspondence. It's
what she would have done at Montaine House. But a quick
glance at her trunk reminded her she hadn't brought along a
lap desk, nor stationery and ink.

Once again, she was impressed by the staff of the Soho
Club, for when she had emerged from her room that morning, the scents of frying bacon and coffee leading the way to
the chair in which she currently sat, she asked the footman
who waited on her if there was a stationery shop nearby.

"What do you require, my lady?"

"I wish to write a letter," she had replied, and then watched in wonder as the footman disappeared for only a moment and then returned with a sheet of fine parchment, a sharpened quill, and an ink pot.

"If you need more paper, you need only ask," the footman said as he delivered her breakfast.

*So, my dearest Adeline, having begun my day with a most wonderful pot of chocolate and the accoutrements to write this letter, I find I am without suitable words to thank you for your recommendation of the Soho Club. Without your assistance, I wouldn't have even known there was a club specifically for women...*

At the muted sounds of nearby conversation—the voices were decidedly male—Elaine lifted her head and surveyed the dining room. She blinked when she discovered there were indeed men in residence. Two *gentlemen*, to be exact, given their manner of dress and their manners.

Neither were paying her any mind, although they both had their backs mostly to her, given how they were seated at a table farther into the dining room.

When she didn't recognize their voices—not that she was eavesdropping, exactly—she returned her attention to the letter to finish it.

*... and gentlemen of good breeding.*

*I hope this letter finds you in good health and that Morganfield appreciates what you've been plotting for your next foray into his bedchamber. Your ideas for pleasing the marquess have been an inspiration to those of us who wanted to ensure we weren't competing with a mistress for our husband's attentions.*

This last line was a lie, but she didn't want anyone knowing that Montaine had most certainly employed a mistress. He had been rather discreet about it, for she never overheard any gossip in Mayfair nor had she read any hints of it in *The Tattler*.

Allowing a wan grin, she signed the letter with her given name and set aside the pen and paper to concentrate on her breakfast.

A twinge of regret at having written that last line in the letter had her thinking she might scratch it out prior to sending it to Adeline.

It was easy to make others believe all had been well with her and Montaine when he'd been alive. That they had enjoyed a marriage of affection, and with it, the marriage bed.

They had at one time. Gabriel Denberg had courted her with the same enthusiasm Octavius, Duke of Huntington, had courted her sister, Jane. Bouquets of flowers, rides in Hyde Park, waltzes at balls, nights at the theatre. Once she'd given birth to Graham and later, his brother, Gabriel, though, her husband returned to the mistress he had employed prior to their marriage. Or, at least, she was fairly sure he had.

Not willing to break her own vows, Elaine had to be satisfied with only an occasional visit by Montaine to her bedchamber. When she had asked him why he kept a mistress when she was such a willing wife, he merely shrugged, said that he loved her dearly, but that he required variety.

The last thought had her turning her concentration on the papers she had brought with her to the dining room.

Her husband's last will and testament.

The solicitor had read the document aloud the week

after Montaine's death, of course. The day she and her sons were gathered in the Montaine House study. But she had bristled at his continued paraphrasing, at how he seemed to skip over entire sections of the text, treating her as if she didn't have a brain. Even after she informed him she had seen to the earldom's accounts for twenty years—Montaine had never trusted his man of business—the odious creature continued to direct his attention to her sons.

"Don't take it personally, Mother," Graham had said once the solicitor took his leave—and a cheque for one-hundred pounds. "He's not used to dealing with women."

"Dismiss him immediately," she had demanded. "And turn your affairs over to Barton in Oxford Street," she added, referring to Andrew S. Barton, Esquire. "He has seen to the Ludlow affairs since before I married your father."

Although Graham hadn't responded one way or the other, she was fairly sure he hadn't hired Barton.

In the meantime, she had a copy made of the document —the one she now held—and was reading it from the beginning when a masculine voice asked, "Might I sit with you, my lady?"

Elaine glanced up, and then watched in surprise when the owner of the voice pulled out the chair next to hers and settled himself into it.

# CHAPTER 2
# SECOND THOUGHTS

*E*laine's eyes rounded at the man's audacity—she hadn't had a chance to respond to his, "Might I sit with you, my lady?" before he simply took a seat—and she was struck by two thoughts at once.

He was handsome. Terribly handsome. He wasn't particularly old, but his days as a young buck were long past. Dark hair, trimmed rather short, was graying at the temples and matched the eyebrows that framed eyes of a deep blue. His nose was straight, a sign he hadn't engaged in bare knuckle boxing at either his university or Gentleman Jackson's boxing saloon. But what caught her immediate attention was his lips and how there was the hint of a quirk in one corner, as if he was in possession of an amusing secret.

Well, if he was, she was sure it was at her expense.

The second thought was that she didn't know the man. At least, she was fairly sure she had never met him before.

Elaine glanced around the dining room. For a moment, she thought of returning to her room. Curiosity had her remaining in place, though.

"If you must," she finally replied.

"Oh, I must," he responded.

Elaine stared at him before she asked, "Pardon, but do I know you, sir?"

He angled his head to one side. "I wish that were so."

Momentary fear had her collecting her papers. "If you'll excuse me..." She started to stand, as did the stranger.

"I didn't mean to interrupt," he murmured.

"And yet you did," she countered, a hint of annoyance sounding in her voice.

She noticed how he had the good graces to at least look as if he regretted his action before he said, "Please. Don't go. Finish your reading. I can wait."

Leaning against the chair for support, she scoffed. "Wait? For what?"

"You."

Elaine scoffed again. "Sir, I do not know you—"

"Edward, Marquess of Delton." He bowed and reached for her hand, lifting it to his lips. "Your servant, my lady."

Habit had Elaine executing a perfect curtsy even as her hand was still in his possession. His gentle hold sent a jolt of awareness up the entire length of her arm. "My lord," she replied.

When she didn't offer her name, he said, "You are Lady Montaine, are you not?"

Her eyes widened. "I am. How did you—?"

"I asked," he admitted, his gaze darting briefly up the stairs. The door to Mrs. Skarsgard's office was directly across the corridor at the top. "Our hostess was most obliging."

"Oh, was she?" Elaine replied, deciding she would amend her letter to Adeline and never again use her card to gain admittance to the Soho Club.

"Please, do not blame her. I can be very demanding when I'm of a mind to be," Edward replied.

"Demanding?" she repeated. Elaine swallowed before she lowered her eyes. "I suppose your station affords you the right." She did her best to hide her annoyance, not wishing to displease the lord.

"I may have played the 'marquess' card," he admitted, somewhat sheepishly. He seemed unsure of what to do next. What to say. He motioned to the will. "Please, do finish reading your document. As I said, I can wait."

"For what, exactly?" Elaine countered. She had a mind to collect the letter and will and rush off to her room, but she knew he would simply follow her. Probably stand outside the door until she... what?

*What did he want?*

As if he could read her thoughts, he said, "A few moments of your time."

## CHAPTER 3
## A MARQUESS MAKES
## HIS CASE

*E*dward held his breath as he considered how Elaine Denberg, Countess of Montaine, might respond. Although he hadn't expected her to simply fall into his arms, he hadn't thought she would be so suspicious of his motives.

He had spent the night before in his room in a state of frustration. Having come to the Soho Club in order to review the ledgers of his marquessate—he was fairly sure his man of business was embezzling from his accounts—he had been unable to concentrate on the numbers. His mind was consumed with images of the countess.

Before her arrival the afternoon prior, Edward hadn't been aware of her. From her manner of dress, he knew she was either a member of the *ton* or the wife of a wealthy merchant. From the way she held herself as she was escorted to her room—only two doors from his own—he thought she was to the manor born.

But it was her expression of sadness—grief, even—that had him wanting to provide solace. Wanting to provide protection. A sympathetic ear should she wish to share the reason for her depression.

Unable to concentrate on his matters of estate, he had undressed. Slipped into a bed with downturned linens as soft as he imagined her to be.

And then imagined her.

He had taken his member in hand and brought himself to a quick and satisfying completion by merely thinking of her.

So when she had asked him, "For what, exactly?", he couldn't admit the real reason.

That he wanted her.

Wanted to erase the sadness in her eyes. Wanted her to share his bed. Wanted to make love to her. Wanted to hold her in his arms for an entire night.

Given how she featured in his vivid dreams, he awoke hoping he might dream of her again and again.

Unable to sleep late despite the comfortable bed, he had emerged from his room for an early breakfast and nearly collided with Henry Tuttlebaum, Viscount Whittingham.

"In town for the holiday?" he had asked Henry. The viscount was taller than even him, but far leaner. There were times when he thought Henry might topple over given his spindly legs and odd gait.

"I am. For the first time in an age, my sister and Middleton are actually spending Christmas together here in London," he replied, referring to George, Earl of Middleton, and his countess, Laura. "His townhouse is entirely too small for all of us, and so I've come here. Can't say I mind, since the food is much better."

Edward had grinned even as he briefly remembered holidays spent in a crowded house. As chaotic as those days had been, he missed them terribly. Perhaps when his last surviving son and heir finished his schooling at Oxford, they could spend a holiday with his late wife's family in their country manse. "Join me for breakfast?" he had asked then, realizing he couldn't bear to be alone with his thoughts.

"Of course. What brings you to the Soho Club?" the viscount had asked as they made their way down the stairs and into the dining room.

What indeed?

*H*e would normally be ensconced in his country estate in Dorchester, traveling there by coach once the autumn sessions of Parliament were finished. This year, he received a letter from his banker suggesting his accounts seemed 'off'. But then, weren't everyone's at the end of a year that featured more rain than usual? Fewer crops? Colder temperatures?

His holdings included a few coal mines, so the Delton marquessate was better off than most, but the fact that Sir William would actually take the time to write a letter had Edward rather alarmed.

And so he had asked Pickering, his man of business, to bring all the Delton ledgers to his South Audley Street townhouse. The weasel had done so, but his nervousness had Edward growing suspicious. When he had put forth a few questions regarding a couple of the accounts, the man had sputtered and said he would have to review his notes. That he couldn't remember such details.

"I pay you to know those details," Edward had countered, scoffing. When Pickering couldn't—or wouldn't—answer, Edward inhaled deeply and asked about other inconsistencies he had discovered in only the few moments he'd had one of the ledgers opened on his massive mahogany desk. When it became apparent Pickering hadn't been doing the business of the marquessate, Edward ordered him to leave. It was when Pickering asked about a character that Edward knew something was very wrong—he hadn't fired the man, exactly. He had merely asked him to leave.

"Before I quit your employ, sir, might you be so kind as to provide a character?" Pickering asked.

Edward merely shook his head and told the man he should be glad he wasn't going to tell everyone in the *ton* what he had discovered. Within moments, he had a footman delivering a note to Sir William asking that Pickering's access to his account be rescinded.

Two days later, and he was still trying to sort the degree to which Pickering might have ruined his marquessate. Unable to concentrate on the matter in the study at his townhouse, Edward had dug up the Soho Club card buried in one of his desk drawers, ordered his valet to pack a bag for him, and he had made his way to the exclusive club.

So when Viscount Whittingham asked what brought him to the Soho Club, Edward merely shrugged. "A change of scenery is all. And better food." During their breakfast of coddled eggs, several rashers of bacon, toast points slathered in butter and topped with jam, and coffee, their conversation turned to matters of estate.

"Tell me, Whittingham, are you aware of anyone in town who is especially gifted in matters of accounting?" He dared not mention the incident with Pickering. The very last thing he wanted was to be the source of gossip. He could just imagine what might happen should a reporter for London's gossip rag, *The Tattler*, discover his situation.

"You mean like a man of business?" Henry countered.

"You misunderstand. I believe I am in need of someone who can audit a ledger." It was at that moment Elaine

Denberg, Countess of Montaine, descended the steps. Dressed in a rather simple pale lavender gown that was almost gray, with her dark hair wound in a chignon at the back of her head, she looked rested. Her sad visage from the day before had been replaced with one of resignation, although whatever the footman had said to her once she reached a table close to the window had her face brightening. Despite the wintery weather outside—once again, snow had begun to fall on the capitol—Elaine looked almost happy.

Henry noticed Edward's attention on the countess and grinned. "Countess of Montaine," he murmured. "I believe she's still in mourning, though." He paused a moment. "Now there was a man of contradictions."

Edward pretended nonchalance. "How so?"

Shrugging, the viscount let go of his fork and leaned closer to the marquess. "From every outward appearance, I assumed those two had a marriage of affection. They always seemed very happy together at all the Season's entertainments. So imagine my surprise when I learned Montaine kept a mistress," he whispered hoarsely. "As if he couldn't be satisfied with just one woman." This last was said as if Henry was jealous of the late Earl of Montaine.

"It's not so unusual to have both," Edward had commented, although he remembered thinking what a fool Montaine had been to leave such a lovely creature alone. Until then, he hadn't even considered the possibility she might have had her own paramour paying a call on her.

He shook his head, not willing to entertain the possibility for even one second.

"It's rather fortuitous that she's here today," Henry commented. "I recall Montaine mentioning quite proudly that his countess saw to his earldom's books." He paused a moment, his gray brows furrowing. "Perhaps she could take a look at yours?" he suggested. "Double check the numbers for you, if that's what you're after."

"A woman?" Edward had countered, struggling to tear his surreptitious gaze from the widow. Memories of the night before, along with the dreams he had experienced, had his cock hardening behind the placket of his Nankeen breeches.

Henry chuckled. "My sister sees to the ledgers for Middleton," he had replied with a shrug. "She's much better at arithmetic than my brother-in-law. I hear most women have to see to their household's accounts, so why not those of an earldom? Or a marquessate?" he reasoned.

So after Whittingham had finished his breakfast and made his excuses—"I have some shopping to do for Christmas,"—the viscount had taken his leave of their table and of the Soho Club.

Emboldened by the viscount's suggestion, Edward had made his way to the countess' table.

"*I*s it true you are particularly gifted in matters of arithmetic?" Edward asked, deciding he best give Elaine a reason for his interrupting her morning. He had thought to mention she had been recommended by Viscount Whittingham, but thought better of it. That would alert her to the conversation he'd been having over breakfast, and he didn't want the skittish countess to hurry off to her room and hide.

Elaine gave a start, her eyes darting to the table where she was sure she had seen him dining with the Viscount Whittingham. Had Henry mentioned her appreciation for numbers? For the rules that had them providing definitive results? She was good friends with his sister, Laura. Perhaps she had informed him. "I am capable of addition and subtraction, multiplication and division. Fractions and—"

"Accounting?" he interrupted. "I am in need of help with some ledgers."

Glancing about to discover they were now alone in the dining room, Elaine frowned. "Ledgers?" she repeated. "Surely you have a man of business?"

He winced. "*Had* one," he acknowledged. "I let him go when I learned he was stealing funds from the Delton marquessate," he explained in a hoarse whisper.

Elaine inhaled softly as her eyes rounded. "Oh, dear. He's been arrested, I hope? Transported?"

About to reply in the negative, Edward instead said, "That will depend on what's discovered in a review of the ledgers. Are you game?"

Her opinion of the marquess entirely different from when he had first joined her, Elaine relaxed and considered the query. "It would be awfully trusting of you to allow me to review your ledgers," she murmured. "You don't even know me."

"But I can trust you, can I not?" he asked, relieved to see she was no longer on her guard. "I'd offer to pay you, but something tells me you might be offended if I did."

Elaine nearly tittered. She'd never been offered pay for anything she'd done in her entire life. "I would not take offense, but I wouldn't accept it, either," she replied.

"Perhaps I could... offer something in return?" he suggested, resisting the urge to add, "Me." After all, he had no idea what she thought of him, although there had been that moment when her breath had caught when he kissed the bare skin on the back of her hand. He was sure there was a moment when she was as aware of him as he was of her. Surely there had been more color in her cheeks than before.

Elaine's gaze darted to the window, where snowflakes still danced about beyond the glass. "I thought to do some shopping today. I have Christmas gifts yet to buy for my two sons."

"Ah. The new Earl of Montaine would be one of them?" he guessed.

"Graham, yes," she acknowledged, sighing as she dipped her head. "And Gabriel is still away at university. If the weather clears, I expect he'll join us for a few days at the house in Mayfair."

From the way she talked about her sons, Edward had the distinct impression she was estranged from the oldest and that the youngest was her favorite.

"I'll be happy to escort you to wherever you'd like to go," Edward offered. "Perhaps it will be warmer later this afternoon? I can have my coach brought 'round. I know it's a huge favor to ask, especially when we've only just met—"

"Oh, I welcome the diversion," she interrupted. "And an opportunity to discover if the manner in which I do the Montaine ledgers matches how a marquessate's ledgers are done."

He chuckled. "Something tells me yours are done better," he murmured. "When and... where would you like me to bring the ledgers?"

Elaine glanced around the dining room. "I've not been here before," she replied. "I'm afraid my room doesn't include a large enough table or a desk of any sort."

"There's a parlor," he murmured. "But I don't recall seeing a desk in there."

"Would you object to me doing it right here?" she asked,

indicating the dining table. "There's plenty of room, and it doesn't appear I would be bothered."

"You wouldn't. Other than by a footman asking if he might bring you tea," he assured her.

She glanced down at the will that still lay on the table, and when she didn't say anything right away, Edward asked, "What is it?"

She seemed reluctant at first, but Elaine straightened and said, "Could I prevail upon you to help me in understanding this document? It's Montaine's last will and testament. Although I was present for the reading, the solicitor skipped over so much of it, I couldn't help but think he was deliberately being obtuse."

Edward's brows shot up. "Hiding something, you think?" he asked, intrigued by her suspicion.

"Or maybe he thought he was doing me a favor," she said with a shrug.

He gave a nod. "I would be honored to look it over," he replied. "It would be good to discover how another peer's estate is handled. I'm always curious if solicitors do their business the same." He glanced around. "But perhaps that could be done in a more private setting," he suggested. "Later this afternoon? After we've done our shopping?" He practically held his breath when saying the last, afraid she might think twice and make her excuses.

"I agree," she replied with a nod, her face taking on a slight blush despite her eight-and-forty years.

"I'll go back to my room for the ledgers," he said as he stood. He chuckled. "They're in green leather bindings, and given my room is entirely green, I may have trouble finding them," he said with a grin.

Elaine tittered. "My room is pink," she countered, "so there's no chance of me losing anything in there."

He sobered. He could think of several things he'd like her to lose when surrounded by pink. Her gown, for one. The pins in her hair for another. When his balls tightened, he knew he had to take his leave. His top coat was of a cutaway design, and there was no hope of it hiding the evidence of his erection.

To take his mind off the thought of her naked and surrounding by pink, his gaze darted to the letter she had written. He could clearly make out the name 'Adeline' at the top. "If you've a letter to send, simply let the footman know. They'll have a courier see to it."

She had nearly forgotten about her missive to Lady Morganfield. "I do. I suppose the ink is dry by now," she replied.

He nodded and bowed before he hurried toward the stairs. By the time he reached his room, his cock had settled down, his carnal thoughts replaced with a growing anticipation for that afternoon's shopping trip.

For once in a very great while, Edward, Marquess of Delton, had something to look forward to.

# CHAPTER 4
# MISMATCHED NUMBERS

*E*laine folded the letter to Adeline and then wrote the address on the outside. Although she had no wax to create a seal, the footman appeared from seemingly nowhere in possession of not only a stick of red sealing wax, but a silver salver bearing a variety of mailing seals.

"I wasn't sure if you preferred to use the Soho Club seal or one of your own initials, my lady," he said as he set down the tray. One gold seal bore an 'M' in a bold script and another an engraved 'E' in a somewhat more feminine flourish.

"I thank you for your thoughtfulness," she said as she lit the wax from the candle in the middle of her table. She held the sealing wax over her envelope until a suitable puddle had formed. Choosing the 'E', she pressed it into the drying puddle and grinned at seeing the result.

"This is ready for the post," she said as she handed the footman the letter. She could imagine Adeline pondering who might have sent the missive given the single letter embossed in the wax.

"I'll have our courier deliver it right away, my lady," the

footman said as he collected the remains of her breakfast and the seals from the table. "Would you like tea?"

Elaine grinned, thinking it odd to be offered tea when she was so used to having to ring for it. "I would, yes."

"I'll return shortly," he said before he disappeared through a door that probably led to the kitchens.

About to return her attention to the will, Elaine stared wide-eyed as Edward descended the stairs, his arms filled with several ledgers. The large books, their pages edged in red, appeared well worn and heavy.

He lowered them to the table, leaving plenty of space in front of where Elaine sat. "They're not all full," he said, as if to allay any fear she might have experienced at seeing their thickness. He took his seat and pulled the top one off the pile, setting it before her.

"Why so many?" Elaine asked, gingerly opening the thick leather-clad cover.

"One for the properties—houses, mostly, which is the one you have there—and three for the coal mines," he replied.

Elaine discovered immediately that the ledger before her was split into several sections, satin ribbon bookmarks separating them. "Townhouse," she murmured, turning the first few pages.

"That's where I live during the Season," he said, "and I believe its entries are current."

Her attention on the individual line items, Elaine drew a forefinger down the sheet, occasionally checking the math before turning her gaze to the facing sheet. She was about to turn the page when the footman appeared with a tea tray laden with cups and a platter displaying several flavors of biscuits.

"I can do the honors," Edward said to the footman,

which had Elaine straightening in surprise. She watched him snag a lemon biscuit from the tray and place it on a saucer.

"My lord?"

He grinned as he poured the tea. "It's the least I can do," he murmured. "How do you take your tea?"

"A little milk. A lump of sugar," she replied, pretending to keep her gaze on the ledger when in fact she was surreptitiously watching his manicured hands. His moves were careful and deliberate, one hand holding the teapot top while the other held the handle. When he poured the milk, he did so very carefully. His handling of the tongs for the sugar suggested he did it often. "Do you usually serve yourself?" she asked, giving up her ruse.

He chuckled. "Every day, twice a day," he replied as he set her cup and saucer safely to the right side of the ledger. "My mother taught me long ago. Biscuit?" He lifted the platter from the salver and tipped it her direction. From the various colors displayed, she realized there were a number of different flavors.

Her eyes rounded. "Is that shortbread?" she asked in awe.

"Shortbread?" he repeated, his brows furrowing as he looked over the selections. "Must be this one?" he asked as he pointed to a disc the color of butter. "What is it exactly?" he asked as he used the tongs to place it on her saucer.

"A Scottish confection," she replied, breaking the biscuit in two before she took a bite. Her eyes rounded in appreciation. "Oh, it's very good." She followed it with a sip of tea before returning her attention to the ledger.

Edward watched her, a wan grin appearing at seeing her reaction to a simple biscuit. How would she react be when he kissed her? When he peeled away the lavender gown and smoothed his hands over her bare skin? When he had her in his bed, wearing nothing more than the bed linens as he made mad, passionate love to her? He had to erase the image lest his cock make itself evident. "Now I must try one," he said, relieved to see there were several on the platter. He bit into one and chewed thoughtfully. "Tastes like... sweet butter with a crunch," he remarked, not as impressed by the biscuit as she had been.

"You say that as if it's a bad thing," she murmured, her gaze having stopped on a figure that seemed wrong. She turned the ledger page back to the one before it, using a forefinger to rest on the ending amount. She turned the page again and looked at the top and shook her head. "Well, this is odd," she whispered.

"Doesn't match, does it?" he asked, finishing off the shortbread with a thought that he'd have to ask his cook if she had the recipe. Despite his initial thoughts about the biscuit, he found he wanted another.

"It's off by one-hundred pounds," she replied, her voice betraying her confusion. She started paging through the ledger, glancing at the ending balance of one page and comparing it to the beginning balance of the next page. Soon, she was into the ledger for his country estate. Then a cottage in Kent—it had only a few pages of entries—and finally into a section marked, 'Horses.'

"Horses?" she asked, her gaze lifting to regard him with curiosity. "You have an estate named 'Horses'?"

He furrowed his graying brows a moment before he realized what she meant. "Not an estate, although they are more expensive," Edward replied with a grin. "My stables," he added. "Those are race horses."

She blinked. "You have more than one race horse?"

He angled his head to one side and briefly wondered if she'd ever attended a horse race. "I have four who are of an age to race," he replied. "And at least another eight who will be in the next year or so."

Sitting back in her chair, the ledger momentarily forgotten, she scoffed. "May I ask why?" she queried, her curiosity apparent.

He chuckled. "As hobbies go, raising race horses is interesting and invigorating. Sometimes unexpected, which only adds to the interest, I suppose," he explained with a shrug. "I especially enjoy selecting the lines for breeding and then discovering if I've made the right choices."

Her brows arched in surprise. "Expensive, too. Especially when..." She turned a page and her eyes rounded. "The numbers don't match."

Stiffening in his chair, Edward gulped. "By how much?" he asked in alarm. He hadn't made it that far in his review of this particular ledger.

"A thousand pounds," she said in a whisper. She continued to page through the 'horses' section, counting the number of times the page balances didn't match from one spread to the next.

"There are several of these mismatched balances," she finally remarked. "Where they occur for the houses, the balances on the next page are always one-hundred pounds less than the page before and one-thousand for your horses."

Elaine continued to turn pages, her brows furrowing before she returned to the beginning of the ledger. She began to count. "Forty-five... forty-six-hundred pounds all told," she whispered.

Raising her head, Elaine discovered Edward's gaze was on her rather than on the ledger. He displayed the oddest expression. "What is it?" she asked, thinking she might have something beyond a biscuit crumb on her lip. One of her hands moved to her face.

"You're especially gorgeous when you're awestruck," he remarked.

She blinked, not sure how to respond to such an audacious comment. "I would expect you to be even more so," she replied.

His eyes darted to one side. "Gorgeous?" he asked in confusion.

"Awestruck," Elaine countered, sure her face was bright red. "And angry. Incensed. Ready to do battle. I almost feared being the messenger of such bad news."

His eyes narrowed despite the slight grin that lifted his lips. "If only all bad news could come from only you," he whispered. He took the hand nearest him and lifted it to his lips.

Elaine gave a start at the shiver that his lips set off beneath her skin. "Why is it you're not angry?" she asked quietly.

He shrugged. "Oh, I am," he replied on a sigh.

"You hide it well."

A sigh of resignation sounded. "I know better than to direct it at those who don't deserve it," he finally said.

She nodded. "Perhaps I should spend some time doing the addition and subtraction. Just to be sure—"

"No need," he replied with a shake of his head. "At least, not for this book," he added as he closed it and pushed it aside. His gaze went to the ledgers for his coal mines, and when Elaine reached for the top one, he captured the hand in his own. "Those can wait," he stated, his gaze settling on the window. "The snow has stopped falling. Let's go shopping."

Elaine turned her attention to the window and grinned when she saw that the sun was attempting to make an appearance. "All right," she agreed. "I'll need to change my gown and fetch a coat and my reticule. Give me twenty minutes?" She refolded the will as she started to push back on her chair.

About to offer his services as a lady's maid as he stood to see to her chair, Edward was prevented from doing so when the footman suddenly appeared with a silver salver. An envelope with 'Delton' written on it was lying in the middle.

"I'll be here in fifteen," he replied, wincing as he took the missive. Gathering the ledgers into a stack and placing the letter atop it, Edward watched Elaine hurry up the stairs, intrigued by how her hips swayed, how their profile appeared through her skirts. He followed at a respectable distance, all the while cursing his cock.

# CHAPTER 5
# ANTICIPATING AN AFTERNOON

*A*ttempting to tamp down her excitement at the thought of spending the afternoon in the marquess' company, Elaine pawed through her trunk in search of a suitable gown to wear. Colors that ranged from gray to mauve had her sighing in disappointment. In a few months, she could return to wearing brighter colors. Until then, she was still in half-mourning.

The thought had her slowing her movements. She hadn't considered being seen in another man's company for the entire time she was married, let alone her nine months of mourning, and suddenly she was excited at spending an afternoon with the Marquess of Delton. A man she hadn't even met before this morning's odd encounter.

What was wrong with her?

*You're especially gorgeous when you're awestruck*, he had said.

*He probably says that to every awestruck woman*, she thought as she pulled a lavender carriage gown from the trunk. She held it up and regarded her reflection in the dressing table mirror. The matching redingote was a bit darker, but not quite purple. At least it was better than gray.

For a moment, she wished she had a copy of *deBrett's* so that she might familiarize herself on the Delton marquessate. She had no idea if the marquess was married or had children. If he did have children, how many did have and how old were they?

Certainly he had an heir.

Who would know?

Reminded that he had asked Mrs. Skarsgard about her, she had a mind to do the same about him.

The thoughts had her pausing in the middle of removing her gown.

Was he married?

Surely Mrs. Skarsgard would know if there was a Marchioness of Delton.

The gown fell to the floor and she stepped out of the puddle of muslin at the same moment there was a knock at the door.

Moving to the bed—she was startled to discover it had already been made—she pulled on her dressing gown and then hurried to the door.

Opening it a few inches, she discovered Lord Delton standing on the other side, his attention on his thumb as it slid along the brim of a top hat he held in his other hand. "Has it already been twenty minutes?" she asked in alarm.

He lifted his gaze and, for a moment, his eyes widened before he glanced away. "Apologies, my lady. I received a note from my butler. I must return to my townhouse forthwith. I shouldn't be long, but it will be more than twenty minutes," he said in a quiet voice. "I promise, I'll return for you, probably within the hour."

Elaine blinked, stunned at the change of plans but heartened he still intended to escort her shopping. "I have a gown all picked out. If you can give me just a few minutes, I can be ready and come with you," she suggested. "Save you the trip back to fetch me?"

Edward was about to beg off, but seeing what he could of her in her satin dressing gown—the door was only opened about four inches—he said, "I could be your lady's maid if you'd like." He waggled his brows in a most teasing manner.

Tittering, Elaine opened the door and stepped back. "Do excuse the mess," she said as she hooked a toe into the fabric of her gown and lifted it enough so she could capture it in a hand and toss it onto the bed. As she grabbed the lavender gown and was about to head to the bathing chamber, she noticed his attention was on the room, his gaze taking in the pink walls and furnishings.

"You weren't joking when you said it was pink," he murmured.

"When you said yours was green, did you mean it was like this?" she asked.

"Yes, but... not the furniture." His gaze settled on the four posters of the bed, the intricately carved wood washed in a pink glaze.

In the bathing chamber, Elaine pulled on the gown. "That surprised me, too," she said, turning to discover Edward watching from the doorway.

He quickly moved to join her, stepping behind her to do up the buttons. When his fingers reached the top fastener, he was forced to push an errant curl aside at the nape of her neck lest it become entangled in the button. He felt as much as saw her shiver in response.

"Sorry," he whispered.

"It's all right," she replied, stunned at feeling his warm

breath so close to her neck. Daring a quick glance in the small mirror above a pitcher and ewer, she checked her hair to be sure the pins were still in place. She had threaded small amethyst earbobs through her piercings earlier that morning and decided they would do for the new gown. "I'll just get my coat and gloves."

Edward followed her out but paused to lean against the door frame. "How much longer will you be in mourning?" he asked.

Elaine pulled some lavender kid gloves from her valise and considered the query before she brought him her coat. "About three months," she replied, as she handed him the garment. "Why do you ask?

He opened the coat, and she slipped her arms into the sleeves. "You don't strike me as a Merry Widow."

Elaine felt her face bloom with color. "Because I am not," she stated. He proceeded to close the frog fastenings of her redingote as if he'd done it a hundred times. "Is that what you thought? That I'd be—?"

"No," he said quickly. "I don't know why I said it, exactly, but I will admit I was pleasantly surprised when you invited me in."

"Well, I certainly didn't want you standing outside my door," she countered in a quiet voice. "For just... anyone to see."

He chuckled. "Forgive me, but there's something I really must do before we take our leave," he said after she had pulled on her gloves.

"Oh?"

Taking advantage of how her lips had formed the 'oh,' Edward lowered his lips to hers and kissed her.

The intimate act did not last long. Neither placed a hand on the other. Their bodies didn't come together in a crushing embrace. If anyone saw them, they might have assumed the two had been married for several years.

But for Elaine, the simple kiss was the first she had experienced in a very long time.

"Are you ready?" he asked, as if nothing had happened.

Elaine stared up at him and swallowed. Although she was sure his simple question referred to their impending shopping trip, she couldn't help but hope he meant far more by it. "Yes. Yes, I do believe I am," she replied as she placed a hand on his proffered arm.

The two took their leave of the pink room and made their way out of the Soho Club.

# CHAPTER 6
# A DETOUR REVEALS MUCH

As if by magic, a black glossy town coach bearing the gold-painted seal of the Delton marquessate on its door pulled up in front of the building at the same moment Edward and Elaine stepped out of the Soho Club.

The guard—it was hard to think of him as a footman given his mode of dress and the manner in which he stood before the entrance—hurried to open the coach door.

Elaine stepped into the blue velvet-squabbed interior, gasping at the elegance on display. Even before she had taken a seat in the direction of travel, she noticed a selection of liquors and crystal glasses tucked into a built-in maple holder on the wall opposite the door. The matching velvet curtains were pulled back and secured with ornate ties. Adorned with satin tassels and trimmed in lighter blue satin, the curtains were finer than those found in most homes.

Taking the deeper seat opposite hers, Edward sat an angle due to his long legs. He lifted his arm to the trap door above and knocked. When the driver's face appeared, he said, "The townhouse," he called up.

"I do hope that whatever requires your attention is not too serious," Elaine commented.

"Well, it is for her," he murmured. "But..." He paused. "I fear everything is these days. I've been assured it will pass with time."

Elaine's eyes widened, sure he was referring to his marchioness. "Are you married, my lord?" she blurted, deciding if he was, she would insist on being let out of the coach right then and there.

Edward blinked. "No," he replied. Then he sighed. "I was, but my wife, God rest her soul, died many years ago. In the childbed," he explained.

Relieved as much as she was embarrassed, she swallowed. "I'm so sorry," she replied in a soft voice. "And the babe?"

His face brightening, Edward said, "No longer a baby. He's at Oxford. Has another year of university before he'll move back to either here or Dorchester."

"He's your heir?"

He nodded. "Indeed. He's sort of lived his life backwards from most, though, but..." He paused, as if he was reconsidering what he was about to say. "It has given him a different perspective. I'm rather proud of him."

Not quite sure what the man meant by his description of his son's life, Elaine thought better than to ask. To her surprise, the coach halted and the door opened only a moment later. "Well, that was fast," she remarked, realizing they were already pulled up to a white stuccoed townhouse with a blue door and matching shutters and window boxes. A green wrought iron fence separated the small front garden from the pavement.

Chuckling, Edward unfolded himself and stepped out of the coach after a footman had seen to helping Elaine. "The club is not far, which is why I chose it over a hotel," he commented.

A butler had already opened the front door, a look of relief on his face. "My lord," he said as he bowed his head.

Even before Edward could reply, screeches and bawling could be heard from somewhere above them. Handing his hat to the butler, Edward dared a glance at Elaine before he hurried into the hall.

Not sure what to do, Elaine followed. Although she normally would have taken a moment to appreciate the fine furnishings and finishes of such a beautiful hall, her attention went immediately to the source of the awful sounds.

At the top of the stairs stood a toddler. The girl, no more than two years of age, was dressed in a white gown made up of several layers of lace and wearing white half-boots topped with lacy trim. Blonde curly hair surrounded her round and red face.

She was obviously upset.

Tears were streaming down her chubby cheeks as her fists flew through the air around her.

"A temper tantrum," Elaine murmured in awe, memories of her boys at that age coming to her in a rush.

"You know what's wrong?" Edward asked hopefully.

She turned to him and then watched as the girl held onto the railings as she made her way down the stairs.

About to head up the steps—she feared for the girl's safety—Elaine was prevented from doing so when Edward lifted an arm in front of her waist. "Don't. Lady Catherine insists on doing it herself," he whispered, as if he were frightened of the curly-haired tyke.

"My lord—"

"Trust me," he said with a pained expression.

Elaine relaxed when the girl made it to the bottom

without falling and then watched in wonder as she rushed towards her. Before she could react, the girl had her arms wrapped around her legs, her cries settling into gulping sobs.

Immediately bending down, Elaine wrapped an arm around the girl's shoulders. "Oh, my darling, whatever has happened?"

The query set off a stream of incoherent babbling punctuated by occasional gasps for air and even more tears. Elaine fished in her pocket for a hanky and wiped the child's cheeks before she pulled her close.

"Oh, my poor dear. Yes, well, sometimes these things happen," Elaine said, pretending to understand. "But they happen for a reason, darling."

The girl sniffled and then said more, none of it in what sounded like English.

"Yes, well, this will pass. You just watch. By morning, it will all be fine. I promise," she murmured quietly. Elaine looked up to discover Edward staring at her in disbelief.

"You understand that language?" he asked in awe.

Elaine stifled the urge to laugh. "A two-year-old's diatribe of distress?" she countered. "Not a bit. However..." She placed her hands on either side of the girl's shoulders and gave her the most sympathetic expression she could. "If I were to guess, she's either in need of her favorite doll—"

"Broken, I'm afraid," Edward whispered.

"Or a nap. Come, you darling creature," Elaine said as she lifted the girl into her arms. Catherine sniffled, but her tears had stopped falling. Her head, however, looked as if it had grown too heavy for her neck. It fell on Elaine's shoulder. She babbled a few words and seemed to snuggle more deeply into Elaine's hold.

"Oh, I can take her," Edward offered.

"I've got her," Elaine replied in a whisper. "Lead the way to her bed, won't you?"

Holding her skirts up with one hand as she supported the girl's bottom with her other arm, Elaine climbed the stairs alongside Edward. "Is her mother not in residence?" she asked quietly.

Dipping his head, Edward seemed reluctant to answer. "She died shortly after Catherine was born."

"Your second wife?" Elaine asked in alarm.

"My son's wife," he corrected her. "When I said John had lived his life backwards, I meant that he fell in love and got married *before* he left for university. They lived in the Delton country estate in Dorchester until her mother... until her mother gave birth and died," he explained in a quiet voice. "John joined me here in London. Brought her nurse, of course, and everything seemed fine until—"

"Until your son went away to Oxford," Elaine finished for him.

Edward grimaced. "I'm a terrible grandfather, aren't I?" he asked. His eyes rounded when he glanced at Catherine. "Is she asleep?"

"She is," Elaine acknowledged with a grin as they reached the top of the stairs. "Is her nurse in residence?"

"Not today," he replied as he led them down the hall to the nursery. "It's her day off."

"Ah," Elaine replied as understanding dawned on her. "So... who sees to her on such days?"

A housemaid emerged from the nursery, her arms laden with laundry. She managed a curtsy despite her burden. "I am so sorry, milord—"

"It's all right," Edward replied. "I'll have Clark contact an agency. See if we can't get another nurse hired."

"Yes, milord." The housemaid hurried off toward the servants' stairs.

Elaine lowered Catherine into her bed and then went about undoing the fastenings on her shoes. "My, such glorious clothes for one so small," she whispered, managing to sound jealous of the lace of the girl's dress. "Was spoiling her your idea?"

Edward bent down, his hand brushing over the toddler's curls. "I was told that as a grandfather, I am allowed," he replied, apparently not about to apologize.

Tittering, Elaine said, "Well, with any luck, my oldest will marry in the next year or so, and I'll have one of these I can spoil rotten." She had the second shoe removed and lifted a light blanket so it settled over the girl.

"Now she looks like a little cherub," Edward remarked quietly.

"She's positively adorable," Elaine agreed, grinning at hearing the tyke's quiet snores.

"Rather a shock considering she was acting like the spawn of the devil only a moment ago." He paused when he noted Elaine's widened eyes. "Pardon my French."

Unable to stifle a chuckle, Elaine quickly straightened and moved out to the corridor. "My lord," she scolded in a whisper of amusement.

Edward grinned as he joined her. He slowly sobered. "I'm going to kiss you," he said.

Not about to deny him, Elaine angled her head and stood on tiptoe, her lips meeting his halfway. This time, he wrapped an arm around her shoulders, as if he needed to hold her up. He deepened the kiss when he realized she wasn't going to protest.

When he finally pulled away, he left his forehead pressed against hers. "I've never been kissed like that," he whispered.

Her face blooming with color, Elaine responded, "If you think I have, you'd be sorely mistaken."

His eyes darted to the side before they once again focused on hers.

Clear green eyes, the color of leaves in the spring. Filled with mischief and so much more.

Did he imagine their longing?

Her lips were red and swollen from his kiss.

Did he imagine their desire for more?

Before he had a chance to consider who might be paying witness to their intimate exchange, he pulled her into an embrace and sighed. "Oh, my lady, you have bewitched me," he murmured softly.

He felt more than heard her purr in response. When he straightened, he found her staring up at him with the oddest expression. "I never thought my penchant for doing arithmetic would have a man enamored enough to kiss me," she whispered.

"I do believe it's more than that, my lady," he replied.

Elaine's eyes rounded. "As I said before, I don't understand baby talk."

He grinned. "Come, let's go see what we can find for Christmas gifts," he suggested.

She nodded, "Might I suggest a new doll for Lady Catherine?"

"My thoughts exactly," he agreed.

The two descended the stairs, grinning when the downstairs maid and butler applauded Elaine as they made their way out the front door.

# CHAPTER 7
# SHARING IS SUCH SORROW

efore they climbed into the town coach, Edward paused and asked, "Where would you like to go?"

Elaine opened her mouth to answer and realized she didn't have a destination in mind. There was a fairly new bazaar with a variety of shops and stalls, but she didn't think she would find anything appropriate for her sons. She thought of Jermyn Street and was about to mention it when Edward straightened.

"I have an idea," he said suddenly. "I doubt I'll find a doll there, but I know I'll find something appropriate for others on my list."

Shrugging, Elaine said, "All right." She was halfway into the coach when she heard him call out, "Rundell, Bridge and Rundell," to the driver.

"A goldsmith's shop?" she asked when he joined her in the coach. Instead of sitting opposite of her, Edward sat next to her, his long legs stretched out in front of him.

Elaine scooted toward the door to give him more room, but he placed a staying hand on her leg. Despite his gloves, the warmth of his hand seemed to penetrate her coat and gown.

When she didn't put voice to a protest, he left his hand where it was. "It's an excellent shop for gifts," he replied. "And it's past time I order a marquessate ring for my son."

"Have you lost yours?" she asked in alarm. She hadn't noticed any rings on his hands when they had been in the dining room at the club, but then she hadn't been of a mind to look for them. His kid glove hid any evidence of rings he might have been wearing at the moment.

"Oh, I have it," he said as he lifted his right hand. "But I thought to give him one. He *is* an earl, you see, if only by courtesy."

"Which courtesy title?" she asked, once again wishing she'd had a copy of *deBrett's* so that she might learn more about his marquessate.

"Stowe," he replied. "He doesn't use it, though. I rather doubt his professors even know he's my son," he commented.

Elaine frowned. Whenever did the son of a peer conceal his true identity? "Does that bother you?"

He inhaled and let the breath out slowly. "I suppose it did at one time. Back when he married," he admitted. "Although his wife was the daughter of a viscount, she wasn't a social climber like so many of her ilk. Sweet girl, actually. I liked her. I think I was as traumatized as he was when she died." His eyes brightened with tears as he spoke, and Elaine was about to offer her hanky before she remembered how sodden it was with his granddaughter's tears.

He lifted his head as if to stare at the ceiling of the coach, blinking a few times. "Catherine will look just like her, I'm sure," he said as he blinked again. "She has her eyes and that comical curly hair."

"Perhaps we can find a doll with the same curly hair," Elaine suggested.

He nodded before he turned his gaze on her. "Yes, let's hope so."

Sensing his moment of sorrow had passed, Elaine asked, "What will you get for your son?"

He shook his head. "That's a good question. Books are always appreciated, but..."

"The ring?" she offered.

"Yes," he agreed. "The ring. And a few books. Mayhap some cuff links and a cravat pin—"

"Oh, my," Elaine interrupted as her grin widened into a smile. "You'll spoil him as much as you do your granddaughter," she accused.

He regarded her with a wan grin. "I could give him the world and John wouldn't be spoilt by it," he remarked.

"Then you have raised him right," Elaine replied.

He nodded, wrapping an arm around the back of her shoulders so he could pull her closer. "And you? What will you buy for your sons?"

Elaine relaxed into his hold, rather liking how his hold seemed to envelope her with warmth. "I have no idea what to get my sons," she admitted. "Men are so hard to shop for at Christmas."

He laughed, the sound a full-throated chuckle filled with amusement. "As if women are any easier," he countered.

Elaine grinned. "Oh, come now. Jewelry is always appreciated," she teased.

"Oh, is it?" he countered. He arched a brow. "I do believe Rundell, Bridge and Rundell are going to do rather well on this day."

Tittering, Elaine wondered if the marquess intended to buy something for her at the jeweler.

She was pondering the possibility when the coach halted in front of the shop in St. James Street.

# CHAPTER 8
# SHOPPING FOR CHRISTMAS

Given the number of coaches that were lined up in front of Rundell, Bridge and Rundell that afternoon, Elaine expected the shop to be especially crowded. So she was pleasantly surprised to discover there were only a few gentlemen lined up at the glass counters and a single older woman perusing the shelves of gifts at the front of the shop.

Although Rundell, Bridge and Rundell was noted for their jewelry, their shop did feature a myriad of silver-plated gifts such as tea sets, snuff boxes, tankards, ice pails, clocks, and candlesticks. When Edward moved to join the other gentlemen at the jewelry counters, Elaine motioned her intention to look at the gifts. She made her way to the farthest shelf and stood in awe as she perused the selections.

As the new Earl of Montaine, her son Graham had taken on the duties of the earldom rather handily, his father having taught him what he needed to know about the entailed properties and how to manage them. Elaine had the impression there was more to it, though. Doing the ledgers allowed her to stay apprised of the financial situation, but she had always felt as if there was more to which she wasn't privy. Some secret her husband had kept, as if he thought he had to protect her from it.

The reminder of secrets had her examining a rather odd silver box. From its outward appearance, it looked as if it was merely a jewelry box with a lid. However, the velvet lined interior wasn't very deep. Examining it more closely, she discovered a secret drawer that opened from the back. Grinning, she decided Graham would appreciate it.

Then she remembered she hadn't told him where she was going when she'd left the house the day before. She hadn't known she would end up at the Soho Club when she took her leave. Didn't know until Adeline Carlington had given her the card and arranged for the Morganfield coach to drop her and her trunk at the club.

She had a thought to send him a note and then wondered if he was even worried about her. Was he still in residence at Montaine House? Or had he regretted his harsh words and returned to his rooms at The Albany?

Shaking the thoughts from her head, she decided to concentrate on finding something for Gabriel. She grinned at imagining what he would appreciate. A fencing foil. She pulled one off the shelf, holding it by its handle as she examined the somewhat decorative guard and the blade.

"Should I be worried for my safety?" Edward asked as he joined her.

"*En guarde*," Elaine teased as she posed with the foil, surprised at how light the weapon felt in her hand. "I'm thinking of getting this for my youngest son."

"You'll have to get one for the oldest, too," he warned.

Her eyes rounded. "I have no idea if Graham knows how to fence," she murmured. "But Gabriel does. He learned at university." She examined the weapon more closely, beginning to question her choice.

"What is it?"

"Would you know if this is any good? As a fencing foil, I mean. Or is it merely for show? To hang above a fireplace in the study."

Taking the foil from her hold, Edward tested the weight from its guard to the button and then gripped the handle. He stepped back to perform an experimental swipe of the blade through the air, watching the tip as he did so. One of his brows shot up. "I would not be embarrassed to wield this in Angelo's Academy," he commented, examining the decorative pommel at the base of the handle.

"So you think it's a good gift for a fencer?"

"It's an excellent gift, even if one wasn't a fencer," he replied with a grin.

Elaine saw how a dimple nearly appeared at the base of his cheek, and she held her breath a moment. "Thank you," she said, when she remembered how to breathe.

Edward chuckled. "Of course. Have you found anything else?"

She pointed to the silver box. "For Graham," she said. "Even though I don't know if all his secrets could fit into it."

Intrigued by her comment, Edward examined the silver box, turning it over and finally opening the lid. It seemed to take him longer to discover the secret drawer than when she had held it. "I see what you mean," he said in awe.

"What did *you* find?" she asked, noticing he had placed a couple of flat boxes on the shelf so he could handle the jewel box.

"Cravat pins for John and a silver bracelet for Catherine. I've ordered the ring, but it won't be ready for a few days," he replied as he took the boxes into a gloved hand.

"Well, you're awfully quick with your choices," she accused.

He shrugged. "Oh, I'm still looking," he replied, his gaze going to the uppermost row of shelves.

Elaine tried to follow his line of sight, but she wasn't tall enough. "What's up there?"

His face lighting up in delight, Edward reached up and pulled a pasteboard box from the top shelf. "If I'm not mistaken—"

Elaine gasped. "A doll," she murmured, recognizing the tell-tale shape of a doll box. She watched as he lifted the lid and angled the box to show her the doll inside. Blonde with blue painted eyes and wearing a gown of primrose muslin trimmed in lace, the doll appeared to be smiling, if only slightly.

"Curly hair," she commented with a grin.

"Both arms are attached," Edward remarked.

"Well, I should hope so," she commented.

"Oh, don't get me started on doll arms," he warned, although his eyes were twinkling in delight. "Clark has had to play surgeon to the last two Cathy decapitated."

Wincing, Elaine angled her head to one side. "Since I never had a daughter, I wasn't aware dolls could suffer so." She glanced around, realizing there were no other customers in the shop. "I'll see to paying for these," she said as she attempted to lift the silver box into one arm and the foil in the other hand while her reticule dangled from one arm.

"You should find something for yourself," he said as he took the jewel box from her. "Try on some rings or neck-laces," he encouraged. "But do be sure not to skewer anyone with that," he teased, referring to the foil.

"I rather doubt I could. It's got that odd little ball at the end of the blade," she replied.

"That's the button," he said. "When that touches your opponent, you score a point."

She tapped the button to his chest. "How many points to win?"

He glanced down to where the button rested against his chest. If there had been a point on the end of a sharper blade, she could have skewered his heart.

From the expression on his face, perhaps she already had.

"Fifteen, if I remember right," he whispered.

Elaine inhaled softly, and then, realizing she still had the button pressed to his chest, she quickly pulled the foil away. "I apologize. I didn't mean to..." She paused, her gaze locked with his.

A grin split his face, and this time, the dimple fully appeared. "It's quite all right," he murmured. "I'm always up for a bit of swordplay."

The oddest sensation shot down Elaine's spine, sending frissons coursing through her entire body. She watched as he moved to the back of the shop, left the jewel box on the counter, gave a nod to the gentleman who stood behind the glass case, and returned to the front to retrieve the doll.

"Do you see anything you'd like to try, my lady?" the shopkeeper asked when she reached the counter.

Although she had no intention of buying anything for herself, Elaine's attention went to a tray of rings that had been left atop the counter. Her gaze settled on a ruby in an intricate gold filagree setting. She handed the man the foil and pointed to the ring as she stripped the glove from her right hand. "I haven't seen anything like that before," she murmured.

"Our newest jeweler is especially gifted at filagree

designs," he replied as he slipped the ring on her fourth finger.

"Oh, dear."

"What is it?" he asked in alarm.

Elaine tittered. "It fits, and it is beautiful, but I shan't be buying it," she said as she shook her head. "I'm supposed to be shopping for my sons. Might I look at your cravat pins, sir?"

He lifted a tray of pins for hats and cravats from the case and placed it on the counter. Boggling at the selection, Elaine was about to give up on choosing two when the scent of Edward's cologne wafted past her nose. She looked up to discover him nodding to a different gentleman behind the counter as he handed the man the doll box.

"I'll see to starting your order now, my lord," the man replied before he disappeared behind a curtained doorway.

"Was that Mr. Rundell?" Elaine asked in awe.

"Indeed," Edward replied, his attention on the cravat pins. "Are you having trouble choosing?"

"I am," she acknowledged. "How did you know what color to get for your son? Or what gemstone to choose?"

He cleared his throat. "When it comes to cravat pins, you want either a diamond or one that is the same color as your waistcoat. So... what colors do your sons wear most often?"

Elaine regarded him a moment before she grinned. She turned to the shopkeeper. "I'd like the emerald, the sapphire, and two with the diamonds, please."

Edward let out a low whistle.

"What?"

"You're going to put my gifts to shame," he teased. "And the Montaine earldom into the red."

She shrugged. "Remember, I am the one who keeps the books," she whispered.

He chuckled.

Once the foil and jewel box were packaged in pasteboard cartons and the pins were tucked into velvet-lined gift boxes, they took their leave of the shop, the clerk carrying the larger boxes.

Elaine didn't notice the shopkeeper slipping Edward an additional box before he stepped into the coach.

# CHAPTER 9
## IF THERE'S A WILL...

With their boxes taking up an entire seat in the coach, Edward and Elaine settled into the squabs on the opposite side. "Where to next?" he asked.

"Do you have others you wish to shop for?" she asked. "I think I'm done."

"As am I," he replied. He was about to tease her about the amount she had spent on her sons at Rundell, Bridge and Rundell, but then remembered she hadn't purchased anything for herself. "You're not in need of any furbelows or fripperies? Ribbons?"

Elaine gasped. "Ribbons," she said. "I think I should like to find some ribbons to decorate the boxes. Make them more festive."

Edward concurred but then grimaced. "I fear I am unfamiliar with ribbon shops. Where should I have my driver take us?"

She considered the options. "Harding, Howell and Company," she replied. "In Pall Mall." Although the draper shop carried far more than what she was after, it was large and offered an opportunity to do some walking.

About to knock on the trap door, Edward didn't have to when the driver called down, "Where to, my lord?"

"Harding, Howell and Company."

"Very good, sir."

As the coach lurched into motion, Edward regarded Elaine with a look of bemusement.

"What is it?" she asked.

"I'm trying to sort what I'm going to use as an excuse to keep you in my company for the rest of the day."

Elaine gave a start and then stared at him with a look of awe. "Would it help if I said you didn't need a reason?"

One of his hands covered one of hers, and he pulled it onto his thigh. "It would, of course."

"You don't need one. Besides... there are ledgers I said I would review," she remembered.

"I promised to read the will," he countered.

Elaine inhaled softly. "Yes. The will." The reminder of the document had her good mood darkening, and Edward immediately noticed.

"What is it about that will that has you so worried?" he asked gently.

She shook her head. "I'm not sure. Maybe it's just because the solicitor didn't read the entire document out loud. The week after Montaine died." Edward furrowed his brows, and in the light from the coach windows, Elaine could see there were gray hairs sprinkled amongst the black brows. She hadn't noticed them before. Now she wondered how old he was. He had a grown son. *Surviving son*, he had said, which implied there was at least another. He could be her age or older.

"How is it you came to that conclusion?" he asked, unaware of how she studied his features. He had been pondering how she referred to her late husband by his title rather than by his given name.

Elaine scoffed. "Because I could see him reading a few lines here and there and then turning the page without saying anything," she explained. "He talked only of those matters directly affecting my sons and me."

"They could simply be matters of estate," he suggested. "Unentailed properties—"

"Every property is entailed," she stated. "Remember, I keep the ledgers for all of them."

"At least, those you know about," he countered.

When her gaze didn't waver, Edward realized why she was so suspicious. "Ah. So you think there *are* unentailed properties?" he guessed.

"Mayhap," she replied on a sigh. "And others who benefited from his death but were not mentioned by the solicitor."

He considered this comment and realized what she meant. "Probably his valet," Edward murmured. "Any other trusted servants. Your butler, perhaps?"

She shrugged. "Possibly. I didn't get that far whilst reading the will this morning."

"Because I interrupted you," Edward said as he began to understand why it was she had seemed so annoyed with him.

"Yes," she affirmed, her face blooming with color. "But I really didn't mind. Not after the introductions."

He chuckled. "You had every right to be suspicious of me and my motives," he offered as the coach came to a halt. A quick glance out the window showed they were in Pall Mall.

"I wasn't suspicious."

He grinned as a footman opened the coach door. "Annoyed, then," he offered.

Unable to reply, Elaine stepped out of the coach and waited until Edward emerged, touched when he offered his arm. "Perhaps," she admitted.

They stepped into the department store, Edward pausing when he saw how large it was. "Oh, my," he breathed.

"The ribbons are this way," Elaine said as she indicated an area to the right.

"How is anyone supposed to find what they're looking for in here?" he asked in awe as they passed display upon display of various and sundry items.

"Well, there are employees one could ask," Elaine replied, "but sometimes it's more satisfying to simply find things without knowing exactly what you're looking for."

He gave her a look of disbelief. "You say that as if that is how you shop here."

She shrugged. "I usually have something in mind," she said. "Fabric and trims, or fripperies. I don't come intending to simply wander around."

From the way he slowed his steps, Elaine wondered if she had said something wrong. "My lord?"

Edward gave a shake of his head. "Call me Edward, won't you?"

She gave a start. Despite the amount of time they had spent together that morning, he hadn't given her permission to call him by his title. Now he was telling her she could call him by his Christian name. "You may call me Elaine if you'd like," she offered.

Staring at her, Edward said, "Elaine," in a whisper. He moved closer and seemed about to say something when a young woman approached them. When she noticed their manner of dress, she curtsied. "May I be of assistance?"

Elaine turned her attention on the shopgirl. "Thank you, but I'm only here for ribbons." She waved toward the wall where spools of ribbons were on display.

"Happy Christmas," the girl said before she bobbed her head and hurried off.

Turning her attention back to Edward, Elaine inhaled softly. He was staring at her, much like he had when he had kissed her earlier that day. "Not here, Edward," she whispered, her gaze darting about, as if she feared someone might be watching them.

He gave a start. "Apologies."

She stared up at him, a wan grin appearing. "Although... I wouldn't mind..." Pausing, she glanced around. When she didn't see anyone looking in their direction, she stood on tiptoe and kissed him on the lips. "In the coach," she whispered.

Edward blinked. "You minx," he accused. But a huge grin brightened his features.

Once again, the dimple appeared, and her cheeks bloomed with color. "*Ribbons*, Edward," she whispered. Before he could respond, she hurried to the ribbon display and plucked a spool of sapphire blue satin and another of a bright green from the rack. "What color would you like for the doll's box?"

"Red, I should think," he replied, his gaze going from the thin ribbons to the ones that were much wider. When he saw that she had fairly wide spools, he took down the bright red one that matched in width. "The color of holly berries."

"Will you have greens brought into your townhouse on Christmas Eve?" Elaine asked. "If so, you can use the red ribbon on the sprays for your fireplace mantels and the railings of your stairs."

Edward glanced down at the spool of ribbon. "I've never

done that in London," he said. "In fact, we've only ever done the hanging of the greens at the country estate."

The mention of a country estate reminded her his was in Dorchester. The Montaine was there as well, but she didn't know the distance between them. "Do you usually spend Christmas in Dorchester?" she asked, glancing in the direction of the gold ribbons.

He nodded. "We do. This will be our first Christmas in London."

Elaine inhaled softly. "If it snows, the city is especially nice," she said. "At night, the windows of all the shops are decorated with candles and greenery. Gold ribbons and silver bows—"

"Will you help me? With the hanging of the greens?"

Blinking, Elaine stared at him. She thought of Montaine House. Surely the butler would see to sending a footman or two to acquire the evergreen bows. Graham would know what to do. He had helped with the hanging of the greens from the time he was tall enough to reach the mantels. It would be odd not to help decorate the house, but until she and Graham could clear the air betwixt them, she decided it would be best if she stayed away.

"I will," she replied with a nod. She indicated the roll of ribbon he held. "We'll need more than what you have there, though," she warned.

His expression changed slightly. "Different widths?" he guessed, noting how he had the only spool of wide red ribbon.

"We'll make them work," Elaine said as he pulled two more spools from the display. She helped herself to a gold metallic length of ribbon. "This will do nicely for one of my boxes."

Although he was half-tempted to look over the other offerings in the large store, Edward decided he wanted to spend more time in Elaine's company—alone. "Let me pay for these, and we'll be on our way," he offered as he took her ribbons and headed toward the counter.

Elaine watched him go, her gaze following his retreating back as she recalled how she had kissed him in the middle of the store.

What had she been thinking to do such a thing? And then to suggest he could return the favor when they were in the coach?

Whatever did he think of her?

Perhaps he wouldn't remember what she had said. She realized there was only one way to find out.

When she could finally get her feet to move to join him at the counter, he grinned down at her as the shopkeeper completed his receipt. He paid with coins from his waistcoat pocket and accepted the tissue-wrapped package with a nod.

When he offered his arm, Elaine placed a hand on it and held on until he helped her into the Delton coach. "I must make one more stop," he said before he disappeared to speak with the driver.

A moment after he stepped into the coach, he had her pulled onto his lap. Elaine relaxed into his hold, reveling in how he kissed her with utter abandon. Despite her thoughts that he did so because he intended to make her his mistress, she returned each and every one of his kisses. How could she not? For the first time in her life, she felt desired.

When the coach halted in Doctors' Commons, Edward reluctantly ended an especially passionate kiss. "I look forward to doing that again. If I'm allowed."

Elaine was sure she looked like a wanton, what with her

eyes glazed over and her lips swollen from his kisses, but she found she didn't care. Embarrassment flooded her after a moment, though, when she realized he expected her to get up from his lap. She didn't think she had the strength, let alone the will to stand. She would have been happy to stay right where she was for the rest of her life.

Before she could make the attempt to stand, he slid one arm beneath her knees and the other behind her shoulders. He lifted her and moved her onto the bench, managing an expression of regret when he said, "It's only a matter of business. I shouldn't be long." He kissed her once more on the forehead.

Elaine inhaled softly, realizing he meant to leave her in the coach. "Then I'll start decorating my boxes," she said as she searched in her reticule for her sewing scissors. She watched as the door opened and he took his leave. Turning her attention to the package of ribbons, she set about wrapping them around the pasteboard boxes, tying the ends into decorative bows.

Fifteen minutes later, Edward reappeared, looking happier than when he had left her. "Now, you do realize you'll have to do the same to my gifts?" he asked, after he had admired her handiwork.

"I'd be happy to," she replied. About to reach into the tissue for one his rolls of ribbon, she paused when he said, "You needn't do it now. I was hoping you would remember what we were doing before my appointment."

Elaine's eyes rounded. "Are you referring to when you were kissing me?"

"Oh, and here I thought you were kissing me," he teased.

He held her in his arms and kissed her quite thoroughly all the way to the Soho Club.

Although the swordplay he had referred to earlier would have to wait, and despite the layers of fabric that separated them, Elaine was well aware of his sword as it made its presence apparent against her hip.

## CHAPTER 10
## ... THERE ARE RELATIONS

*An hour later, at the Soho Club*
Resuming their places at the same dining table they had occupied earlier that morning, Elaine and Edward ordered tea. Two of the coal mine ledgers were stacked near Elaine while she had the third open in front of her.

Meanwhile, Edward held the multipage copy of Montaine's will, his gaze darting back and forth across the front page as he read the even script.

"Who made this copy?" he asked as he turned the page.

Elaine glanced up from the ledger, an empty quill held over one of the entries. A footman had delivered an ink pot and pen as soon as they sat down, apparently deciding they would be in need of them. "I hired a clerk to do it from the original. Graham keeps the original will in the desk in his study, so it was easy to arrange the copy," she explained.

"You trust the clerk?"

The query had Elaine giving a start. "He was recommended by Morganfield," she said in a quiet voice, referring to David Carlington, Marquess of Morganfield.

It was Edward's turn to react in surprise. "Oh, well, I

must say, this clerk has most excellent penmanship," he remarked.

Elaine grinned and returned her attention to the ledger. When the tea arrived, Edward once again saw to pouring it. He made sure Elaine had a shortbread biscuit on her saucer when he set the teacup to her right.

"You're spoiling me," she murmured, not taking her eyes off the figures she was reviewing, mentally adding and subtracting numbers before turning to the next page.

"Someone has to," Edward replied, his voice sounding far away. "Montaine certainly didn't."

Pausing in her review, Elaine looked up and stared at Edward. When he finally met her gaze, she said, "Whatever do you mean?"

He scoffed. "Was the earldom in financial straights when he wrote this will?"

Elaine blinked. "There were a few years when the crops didn't fare well—like this past year, of course—but the coffers have always had more than enough to cover the expenses," she replied. "What have you discovered?"

Leaning back in his chair, Edward sighed. "That your late husband thought you could live on very little for the rest of your life." He made the comment with a hint of contempt.

"Well, I am really rather thrifty," Elaine remarked.

"From our time in the draper, I would concur," he replied.

"Why do you say it like that?" Her attention was entirely on him, the ledger forgotten.

"We were in a rather large shop with all manner of... *stuff*," he stammered. "And yet you didn't take a single moment to look at anything but the ribbons."

"Well, that's all I was in need of," she countered.

"But what did you *want* to look at? What would you have liked to buy?"

Elaine blinked. "Ribbons," she answered with a shrug.

"You weren't the least bit tempted to look at the gowns or the fripperies? Hats or..." He paused to remembered what else he had seen in the store. "Fabric?" He regarded her as if he couldn't believe what she was saying.

She sighed. "I've another three months of half-mourning, my lord," she reminded him.

"Edward," he corrected her. He glanced around to confirm they were the only ones in the dining room. "Call me Edward when we're alone, won't you?"

Her eyes rounding slightly, Elaine nodded. "All right." She inhaled softly. "I promise, Edward, when I am done mourning, I will shop for fabric. I will have my modiste make me a suitable wardrobe for the Season." She sighed. "And hope that I haven't been completely forgotten when invitations are drawn up for the Season's entertainments."

"I will be sure you are not," he said, his attention once again going to the will.

When he didn't offer the reason for his original comment, Elaine asked, "Pray tell, what makes you think Montaine didn't afford me a suitable allowance?"

Edward shrugged. "When my marchioness was still alive, I saw to it she had an allowance that was three times what Montaine has bequeathed you."

Elaine inhaled softly. "Did she actually spend it all?"

He guffawed. "All of it, and sometimes more," he replied with a shrug. "But I did not mind. She was a good wife and an even better marchioness."

Angling her head to one side, Elaine felt a pang in her chest. "You miss her," she said, not making it a question.

Edward blinked and tried hard to maintain an impassive

expression. "For the first few years after her death, I was devastated," he affirmed. "After a few more, I accepted it and moved on."

"And now?"

His gaze settled on her, his eyes darkening with desire. "I have a plan for the future," he murmured. "I'll share it with you later if you'd like."

Reminded of how he had kissed her with such abandon in the town coach, Elaine inhaled softly as a shiver passed through her. "I would like that," she replied. Dipping her head, she returned her attentions to the ledger and continued with her review.

Nearly a half-hour passed in silence before Edward asked, "How well do you know Viscount Whittingham?"

Elaine gave a start. "I don't. Not really," she replied.

Edward furrowed his brows. "You know *of* him?"

"Well, of course. He occasionally paid a call on Montaine at the house," she said. "I am friends with his sister, Laura, but we only see one another on a few occasions since she's rarely in London. She's Middleton's countess." Her brows furrowed with concern. "Why do you ask?"

Holding the third page of the will, Edward angled his head to one side and recited, "To Henry Tuttlebaum, Viscount Whittingham, I bequeath the entirety of my art collection which can be found in the salon adjoining the master suite of Montaine House and an allowance of five-hundred pounds a year to use towards its conservation."

Elaine stared at Edward for several seconds before she swallowed. Tears were soon streaming down her cheeks.

"Elaine," he whispered, quickly pulling a handkerchief from his pocket and offering it to her. "Why ever are you crying?"

She took the square of linen and quickly dabbed her

cheeks. "He claimed he was resuming his arrangement with his mistress. After Gabriel was born," she whispered. "I never had any reason..." She paused to suppress a sob. "... to suspect otherwise."

Edward practically growled as he thumbed through the two remaining pages, looking for a mention of a woman. When he couldn't find anything, realization slowly dawned. He lifted his head and cursed softly. Noticing the footman hovering near another table, he waved him over and said, "Bring a bottle of brandy. Two glasses."

"Right away, milord."

After the servant disappeared, Edward leaned toward Elaine. "Did you... did you suspect him of being a...?" He didn't finish the query, not sure she would know about homosexuals.

She shook her head. "Well, not for many years," she whispered. "When Whittingham would come to the house, they always went upstairs. To Montaine's salon," she added, sniffling.

Edward winced. "What sort of art did Montaine have on display in his salon?"

Attempting to stifle a sob, Elaine's face bloomed with color. "Nudes," she replied finally. "Although there are paintings of both men and women," she murmured.

"Has Whittingham come to collect them?"

Elaine blinked several times. "I've no idea," she replied. "If so, I'm quite sure he would have arranged it with Graham," she added. She took a deep, shuddering breath. "Will you report Whittingham to the authorities?" she asked, her eyes widening in alarm. Before Edward could reply, she added, "Please don't."

Edward's brows drew together, a fold of skin forming

between them. "I shan't say a word, although I must warn you that there are some who already suspect him."

Elaine gasped. "And Montaine? Did anyone—?"

"I never heard anything about him," Edward quickly assured her. "You needn't worry about his reputation." He was about to say more, but the footman was on his way back to their table, his silver salver bearing a bottle of French brandy and two glasses. He set the salver on the table.

"I'll serve," Edward said, giving the footman a wave as if he was dismissing him. The young man bowed and hurried off.

Edward poured the brandy and then offered a glass to Elaine. "Drink. It will help dull the shock of all this," he urged.

Taking the glass, Elaine sniffed its contents before she took an experimental sip. Warmth raced down her throat, thawing the chill that had settled inside her. She visibly relaxed but then nodded toward the pages he still held. "Is there anything else you've discovered?"

He shook his head before he took a sip of his brandy. "I've not yet read the rest of it." He paused a moment. "You needn't continue with my ledgers, if you'd rather not."

Her eyes rounded. "Oh, but I will," she replied before she took another sip of the brandy. "My curiosity has me wondering why it is I haven't found a single error in this ledger."

Edward chuckled. "You sound as if you were expecting to," he accused.

"I still am. Although..." She paused and reconsidered. "Perhaps your man of business only embezzled from the household accounts. He probably knew your business ledgers might one day require an audit should your banker... or a business partner ever require it."

"Perhaps," he agreed. "The mines are entailed properties, though. There's no partner involved."

Elaine hummed her response and returned her attention to the ledger. Meanwhile, Edward continued to stare at her. After a time, he returned his gaze to the will and, and taking another sip of his brandy, continued to read. They worked in amiable silence until Elaine looked up from the last page of the ledger.

"Did you find something?" he asked.

"Ten pounds. But the mistake was corrected on the final page in a separate entry," she explained. "It's as if this ledger had been audited." She set aside the book and reached for the next one when the footman reappeared.

"Pardon me, my lord, but the cook is asking if you'd like an early dinner."

Her stomach growling at the mention of food, Elaine gave Edward a hopeful look.

"We would," Edward replied. He took the menu board from the footman and glanced at it before his gaze fell on Elaine. "Would you like to take a look?"

She gave him an impish grin. "I trust you."

A pang had his heart clenching, and Edward took a moment before he gave the footman their dinner order—a long list of dishes that included pheasant. After the servant had departed, Edward said, "My housekeeper sees to the menus at Delton House, so I rarely have the opportunity to choose what I'm to eat."

"What do you order when you eat at Rule's?" she asked, referring to London's oldest restaurant.

"Oysters, of course," he replied. "And whatever game meat might be available. What about you?"

"Pheasant," she said with a grin. She glanced around,

noting a few couples were having tea at the other tables. "I should probably change for dinner."

"You needn't," he said with a shake of his head. "Although some do dress for dinner here at the club, you'll find most do not."

"Why ever not?"

He shrugged. "People come to this club to do whatever they want. Be whatever they want. How they dress for a meal hardly matters."

"Is that why *you* come here?" she asked, curious now about how often he was a guest at the Soho Club.

He inhaled as if to respond and let out a guffaw. "I've not been here very often, and when I've come, it's always to spend some time alone."

She inhaled softly. "Oh, dear," Elaine breathed. "I've been in your company all day. You must be sick of me. If you'd like, I can take my dinner to my—"

"You'll do no such thing," he interrupted. "Stay. Have dinner with me," he encouraged. "And afterwards, we'll enjoy some dessert."

A frisson shot through Elaine as she stared at him, fairly sure he wasn't referring to sweets when he mentioned dessert.

# CHAPTER 11
# DINNER, FOLLOWED BY...

The ledgers and Montaine's last will and testament long forgotten, Elaine and Edward dined on soup and hot bread followed by pheasant, potatoes, pudding, and several vegetables. Their wine glasses were kept filled. As each course appeared, Elaine grinned in delight at the presentation.

Although the Montaine House cook was good at making all the meals for the household, their presentation was not anything special. At the Soho Club, the plated dishes came out of the kitchen steaming hot, the foods artfully arranged on china plates.

"Do tell me you come here for the food," Elaine murmured when she had taken her final bite of pheasant.

Edward grinned. "It's definitely a draw," he admitted. "As is the bed."

Elaine gave a start. "Yours is comfortable, too?"

He chuckled. "I tried to buy it, but Mrs. Skarsgard said it's not for sale."

Tittering, Elaine regarded her nearly empty plate. She

had eaten most of what had been offered and was pleasantly full. "I can't imagine eating dessert right now."

"We can wait," Edward suggested.

Although she had avoided the topic during their dinner, Elaine was curious as to what the marquess might have discovered when he finished his review of the will. She brought up the topic when he didn't offer any comment on it. "Pray tell, did you find anything else in the will? Any other... surprises?"

He shook his head. "Your younger son has a suitable allowance for his position. You seem amenable to your pittance of an allowance, although I would encourage you take up the matter with the current earl," he murmured. "As long as your oldest son follows the terms of the will—it seems he is the executor—the staff at Montaine House will be paid appropriately," he explained. "There isn't a requirement you move to the dower house, but—"

"What's this?" Elaine asked in alarm.

Edward blinked. "The dower house. There's a property set aside for you to live in, with a suitable household staff and funds for its upkeep, for when you decide to vacate Montaine House."

Elaine shook her head. "I know nothing about it," she whispered. "Graham hasn't said a word." Her eyes rounded. "Where is it?"

Reaching for the folded document, Edward pulled out a page and quickly perused it. Settling in his chair, he allowed his back to rest against it as a slow grin appeared on his face. "Well, it's not out in the country, if that's what you were fearing," he said.

"Where, then?"

He considered how to respond. "I can take you there. Tomorrow," he said, his gaze going to the window. Falling snowflakes interrupted the blackness beyond the glass, a reminder that Christmas was only a few days away. Returning his attention to Elaine, he couldn't help but notice her stricken features. "My sweeting, it's right here in town. You needn't be worried about leaving your friends."

At hearing his endearment, Elaine raised a brow but relaxed. "Do you suppose I should plan to move out of Montaine House?"

Edward seemed to think on the matter for a moment before he asked, "Did your son marry recently?"

"No," she replied. "At least, if he did, I wasn't made aware of it. He's merely said he intends to court someone."

Scoffing, Edward said, "Well, we're in London, so I have it on good authority that if he *had* wed someone, you would have heard about it. Probably before it actually happened. That, or read about it in *The Tattler*."

Elaine finally allowed a wan smile. "Thank you. For all you did today," she said, waving a hand toward the will.

"Thank *you* for reviewing the ledgers," he replied. "I must say I'm not surprised by what you found in the household ledgers, but I am relieved that my man of business didn't extend his theft to the coal mines."

"They must be doing quite well," she remarked. "Especially this past year, what with it being so cold and all."

He nodded. "Their profits have offset the crop losses," he agreed as the footman appeared to take their plates.

"Would you like your desserts now?" he asked.

Elaine and Edward exchanged quick glances. "Have them delivered to the Pink Room in a half-hour," Edward said. "Along with a bottle of champagne." He held up a finger and added, "And arrange to have bath water delivered to her ladyship's room right away."

"Very good, milord." The footman hurried off to the kitchen.

Gasping—Elaine once again experienced a frisson shoot through her—she stared at the marquess, her face displaying a blush.

"I thought you might enjoy a soak after the day you've had," Edward whispered. "You don't mind, I hope?"

Indecision had her withholding her comment until she finally shook her head. "I don't mind at all, but I must admit I'm surprised you would think of such a thing."

He shrugged. "I might not have had a woman in my life for a very long time, but I do remember those days."

"Fondly, it would seem."

"Indeed. I'll see to putting these away," he said as he indicated the ledgers. "And join you in your room in... say, a half-hour?"

Her heart racing with excitement, Elaine nodded. "I'll be there." She leaned toward him and whispered. "Are you expecting to find me *in* the bath when you arrive?"

Elaine was sure a flush of red colored the marquess' face before he said, "That's entirely up to you, my sweeting."

Left speechless, Elaine accepted his proffered arm and the two made their way up the stairs.

Sure people might be watching, Elaine dared a glance around the club and discovered that if anyone saw them take their leave of the dining room, it wasn't apparent.

## CHAPTER 12
## DESSERT

*E*laine had been in her room for only a few moments, rooting through her trunk for a suitable gown to wear for Edward's call, when there was a knock on the door.

She opened it to discover several footmen bearing pails of steaming hot water. "Pardon, milady, we'll only be a minute," the tallest one said as he led the others into her room's bathing chamber.

"How is it the water is already hot? It was ordered only a few minutes ago," she remarked in awe.

The head footman angled his head to one side. "We always try to have some on hand, milady" he replied. "We don't like to keep our club members waiting." He bowed, as did the others as they marched out, carrying the now-empty pails.

Curious, Elaine hurried into the bathing chamber to discover a full tub and bath linens and a ball of soap set out on a chair next to the tub. A mirror behind the single lit candle lamp reflected the flame, casting the chamber in a golden glow.

Pulling her dressing gown from where the maid had left it folded earlier that morning, she added it to the pile on the chair and quickly undressed.

The Marquess of Delton might be expecting to find her still in the tub upon his arrival—probably hoped she would be—but she had no intention of him finding her in such a state of dishabille.

Elaine returned to her trunk and soon discovered she had nothing appropriate to wear for what she was beginning to realize was a liaison. A prelude to a tumble. And whatever came after that.

Whatever did mistresses wear when they were expecting their men to pay a call?

The thought had flutterbies dancing about in her stomach, although how there could be any room for them, she didn't know. Her pulse sped up at the thought of sharing her evening with the marquess. Montaine had been the only man to bed her, and before that morning, she wouldn't have considered entertaining a male guest, at least not until her mourning period was over.

Now that she had discovered her late husband's secret, she decided she was done with mourning him. With pretending to mourn him.

Glancing about at the pink that surrounded her, she knew she could use it as an excuse for the blush that suffused her body. For some reason, in the light from the two candle lamps, the pink glowed in a far more seductive manner.

Rummaging through her trunk, she paused when a bright fabric appeared among the lavenders and grays. She pulled a simple dinner gown from the trunk, holding it in front of her as she dared a glance in the dressing table mirror. Made of red satin, it was void of ribbons and furbelows. Not sure why her lady's maid would have included the gown when she packed the trunk, Elaine decided it was a happy accident. Despite the fact that it made her blush even more apparent, she decided she would wear it for the dessert course. She draped it over the back of the dressing table chair.

Her anticipation increasing, she stepped into the bathtub and sighed as she lowered her body into the hot water.

How had Edward known this was exactly what she needed? Perhaps it was merely all the wine they'd had a dinner, or the brandy before that, but a sense of relief settled over her as the warmth of the water seemed to permeate her bones.

*Relief.*

Had she really allowed the damned will to affect her so? Now that she knew its contents, she realized it had been the fear of the unknown that had tied her up into knots these past nine months.

She had barely rubbed the ball of soap with a linen when she realized she wasn't alone. Inhaling softly, she turned her attention toward the door to find Edward, his arms crossed, leaning against the door frame. Although he still sported the waistcoat he had been wearing all day, he no longer wore a top coat, and his cravat was missing. The sleeves of his shirt were rolled up to his elbows, exposing tanned forearms.

"Has it already been a half-hour?" she asked in surprise.

He shook his head as he pushed off from where he leaned against the door jamb. He made his way to the tub. "I've no idea. But I couldn't wait," he replied, his eyes darkening when she made no move to cover her nakedness beneath the water. In the dim light, it hardly mattered.

"Our desserts haven't arrived," she murmured, before she

visibly swallowed. With him standing over the tub, he seemed far taller. More imposing.

"Mine is right here," he said as he lowered his knees to the floor.

A thousand sensations coursed through Elaine just then, all of them new to her. How could a man's simple words and steady gaze have her so excited? Goosebumps prickled the skin that wasn't beneath the water. "I don't think there's room in here for you," she whispered, surprised by the disappointment she felt.

He chuckled as he took the ball of soap from her, daring a sniff. "French, no doubt," he commented dryly. He dunked it into the water and then pressed it onto her shoulder and began skimming it over her skin. At times, it dipped beneath the water, over her breasts and belly, along her thighs. Then it emerged to move up over her knees, along her calves, and back down to her feet. All the while, Elaine watched Edward's gaze follow the ball as she did her best not to gasp at his every move.

"You obviously have some experience at this," she remarked, a pang of jealousy ruining the moment. What else could explain his ease at washing a woman's body?

"Not for a very long time," Edward replied, his attention still on his task. He helped himself to a linen, dipping it into the water and then rinsing her shoulders and back with it. "My wife, of course, when she was still alive," he added, obviously noting her look of disbelief.

Elaine relaxed. "You'd make an excellent lady's maid."

He grinned, but there was disappointment in his voice when he said, "I would have made a better one if I'd arrived in time to help you out of your gown."

She inhaled softly. "You can help me into my dinner gown," she offered, well aware her entire body must have had her looking like a lobster, as much from the heat of the water as from her embarrassment.

"The red one?" His head nodded toward the door.

"Do you think it's too much? I'm not sure how to dress for... for whatever... *this* is."

"It's too much," he replied. At hearing her scoff, he added, "I'll allow you to wear your dressing gown and nothing more."

About to put voice to a protest, Elaine couldn't when there was a knock at her room door.

"Pardon me," Edward said as he stood and left the bathing chamber. "Stay right there. I don't want you to take a tumble stepping out of the tub."

When he disappeared from view, Elaine ignored his order and took the opportunity to rise from the tub. As water sluiced from her body, she grabbed a linen from the chair. Glad for its size—unfurled, it was large enough to shield most of her body from hungry eyes—she stepped out of the tub and quickly dried herself.

She didn't have a chance to reach for her dressing gown before Edward returned. He held two glasses of champagne. From his expression, Elaine realized he really was expecting to help her out of the tub. Probably expecting to dry her off, too. "I... I wouldn't have been comfortable with you doing it," she stammered, taking the glass he offered.

Edward winced. "Now you doubt my skills as a lady's maid?" he asked in a quiet voice. He drank half his champagne in a single gulp.

Elaine inhaled softly and struggled to think of what to say. What to do. She took a sip of the champagne. "I'm not completely dry," she offered as she stepped forward. Securing the towel by holding her elbows against her body, she reached out with her free hand and began undoing his waist-coat buttons.

His eyes darkened. "If I'm allowed, I'm about to make you a whole lot wetter." He drained his glass and set it on the dressing table.

He must have known his words would have the desired effect, for Elaine paused in her task, aware of how her pulse throbbed at the top of her thighs. At how damp her curls had become—she had dried them only the moment before. "I don't know what to do," she whispered. "I've never done anything like this before."

Edward's lips captured hers in what she thought would be a crushing kiss, as if she thought he would punish her. But his touch was soft, barely there. His lips seemed to tremble as much as her entire body was threatening to do.

She would have liked the gentle kiss to go on for a few minutes more, but her knees were no longer beneath her, her feet no longer on the floor. Her free hand immediately moved to wrap around his neck as he carried her in his arms.

Elaine stared at him as he easily traversed the space to the bed, settling her on it. He took the glass from her and set it on the dressing table, and when he returned to stand at the edge of the bed, she saw that he had removed his waistcoat.

Supporting himself against one of the posters, he removed his boots and stockings. When he straightened, Elaine swallowed as the silhouette in the placket of his Nankeen breeches made his arousal apparent. The ridge was long and thick, and she quickly glanced away lest he notice her gaze on it.

He noticed.

"It's nothing you haven't already seen on Montaine," he murmured as he stripped his shirt from his torso.

She gasped and pulled the towel tighter around her front.

Edward furrowed a brow. He glanced down the front of his body. "Surely... you've seen a man's bare chest before?"

For a moment, Elaine was speechless. Montaine had always come to her bedchamber wearing a nightshirt. She was sure he left it on during the few times he bedded her. He never stayed with her for very long after he finished, napping only briefly before giving her a peck on the cheek and returning to his own bedchamber.

"On some statuary, I suppose," she replied. "There's a mostly naked man in the Morganfield gardens. But... his chest... well, it looks nothing like yours," she stammered. She tentatively reached out a hand until her fingers touched the dark hair that covered most of his chest. They followed the contours of his torso, down the middle of his stomach to where a whorl of hair disappeared behind the top of his breeches.

Edward sucked in a breath when her fingers skimmed his stomach, partly to stifle a chuckle—he hadn't known he was ticklish there—and partly because he was surprised she would do such a thing.

Elaine immediately pulled her hand away, as if she'd been burned. "I apologize. I—"

"Oh, no you don't," he warned, a slight grin softening the rebuke. His brows furrowed. "What about Montaine? Surely you saw him naked." He couldn't help the scowl that accompanied the query.

She shook her head. "He always wore a nightshirt when he came to the mistress suite. And... he preferred it dark. He always extinguished the lamps before he came to me."

Edward's scowl deepened. "Did he pleasure you?"

Sure her face was bright red with her blush, Elaine swallowed. "When we were first married. He would... touch me." She remembered those moments with fondness, for later she could sometimes feel the frissons that she had experienced by simply thinking of them when she was alone. Until earlier that day, she hadn't felt them in a very long time.

The scowl slowly disappeared from Edward's face, and he said, "I shall do far more than that," he murmured. With his hands and arms, he reached under her body and repositioned her on the bed. She gasped and gripped the bath linen in an attempt to keep herself mostly covered.

"Are you cold?" he asked, obviously concerned.

Elaine's eyes rounded. "No," she replied in a whisper. "This bath linen is rather good in that regard."

He gave her a quelling glance and lifted the linen from her legs. Before she could put voice to a protest, Edward slid his hands beneath the globes of her bottom. He took advantage of her reaction of surprise, to the way she raised her knees in response. He had his body separating them and positioned between them in only a moment. "If I told you to relax, would you?"

Elaine regarded him for a moment before she did his bidding. "What do *I* do?" she whispered, at the same moment he lowered his head between her legs.

"Beg for more, I hope," he said, a moment before his tongue separated the folds that protected her womanhood.

Elaine's immediate reaction was to stiffen. To clench and gasp in surprise. When she glanced down the front of her body and saw his look of admonishment, she sighed. "You surprised me," she accused. "Whatever are you doing?"

Trying to sound annoyed, he said, "I'm attempting to pleasure you by employing an Ancient Roman tactic." He couldn't remain annoyed, though, not when he saw her genuine look of astonishment. Montaine had obviously never learned this particular Roman skill, although Edward sorted he knew of the other. He was fairly sure the late earl had never taught her *that* one, either.

Elaine relaxed, lowering her head to the bed at the same moment he repeated what he had done. Her hips jerked. She tried to close her knees, which had him gripping her hips in an effort to keep her in place, although he didn't seem to mind that his head was caught between her soft thighs.

The second swipe of his tongue over her now-swollen womanhood had the desired effect. Elaine gasped, her back arching in response. He heard her 'oh' of surprise and began to repeatedly flick his tongue over her engorged sex, reveling at how her knees finally relaxed and fell apart, at how she succumbed to his worship of her.

When her ambrosia coated his tongue and he knew she was close to her ultimate pleasure, he suckled her sex between his lips and then his teeth.

He let go of his hold on her and sighed with relief when she cried out. When her series of 'oh's and 'yes's became a plea of 'stop, oh please, stop.'

Quickly unbuttoning the placket of his breeches, Edward stripped the garment from his body and then climbed onto the bed. He barely had her body repositioned before he drove himself into her, his need for her so great, he worried he might come before he could provide her another round of pleasure. He pulled the bath linen from between them, his lips covering one of her nipples before he thrust into her again.

She met his thrust with one of her own, and Edward cursed softly as he could no longer stave off the oncoming pleasure. Two more thrusts and his body stiffened above hers. He threw his head back and growled. He felt her hands move to grip his buttocks. Felt her thighs press against the sides of his. Felt her breasts rise to meet his chest. Heard her mewling and breathy pleas before his pounding pulse drowned out everything but the pleasure that overtook his body.

A moment later, and he knew his arms could no longer hold him suspended above her. Unable to escape her grip, he lowered his body and allowed his head to come to rest next to hers. About to apologize for coming too soon, he felt the ripple of her orgasm along the length of his cock. Felt her stunned inhalation of breath as the waves of pleasure coursed through her abdomen.

He might have sensed more, but he had passed out.

## CHAPTER 13
## LOVE MAKING'S AFTERMATH

"I don't ever want to leave this bed," Edward murmured before he kissed Elaine's shoulder.

A most pleasant shiver passed through Elaine as she lay partly atop him. He was propped against the pile of pillows, his naked body in a pose suitable for the subject of a Renaissance painting. His arms were wrapped around her waist, as if he feared she might escape his hold.

Elaine had no desire to escape, though, her head resting on one of his bare shoulders, her back pressed onto his chest, and her bottom tucked into the bend of his body. "Perhaps they would let you buy this one," she whispered. "And they could just move it to your house."

"With us still in it," he agreed sleepily.

Elaine tittered. "We'd have to pull the linens over us," she said. "Or we'd cause quite a scene, don't you suppose?"

He sighed. "I wouldn't care."

Her head lolled to one side. "Someone will have to bring us food. And chocolate," she whispered.

"True," he responded. "I'd pay them well." He was silent for a time, remembering what he had done when he knew she was asleep after their second round of lovemaking.

Stepping off the bed, he had searched his waistcoat pocket for the ruby ring he had purchased at Rundell, Bridge and Rundell. The one that she had tried on to discover it fit. He repositioned himself on the bed, arranging Elaine's warm, limp body against his until he could slide the ring on her finger. Although she had stirred, she had resumed her slumber a moment later.

It had taken only his slight nod for Rundell to understand that he wanted the ring. For the jeweler to pluck it from the tray, place it in a ring box, and add it to his account.

Retrieving the box from the jeweler without Elaine seeing the transaction had taken a bit more finesse, but once it was safely tucked into his waistcoat pocket, Edward knew she wouldn't be suspicious.

Now he was pondering when they might marry. The special license he had secured from the archbishop the day before would allow them a quick wedding. Given it was Saturday, he knew the earliest they could wed would be the following Monday.

Christmas Eve.

He slid his right hand beneath hers and lifted it, admiring the ruby in the dim morning light from the room's only window. "It's perfect for you," he remarked. "I look forward to seeing you wear it all the time. Especially in that red gown you were going to wear last night."

Elaine gazed at her hand, purring her agreement when she suddenly gasped and escaped his hold. Sitting up in the bed, she held her hand out in front of her as if it were disconnected from her body. "Oh, my," she whispered in alarm.

Edward lifted himself onto an elbow. "What is it?"

She seemed to stare at him a moment, although he knew she was seeing through him. "I was sure I gave it back," she murmured. "I remember trying it on, but I was sure..." She gasped again. "They will think I stole it!"

Chuckling, Edward fell onto his back and wrapped an arm around her waist to pull her down onto him. "You silly goose," he whispered.

Elaine's look of worry slowly cleared. "I *did* give it back," she murmured. "I clearly remember doing so."

"Good thing, too, since I wanted to buy it for you," he replied. At hearing her slight inhalation of breath, he added, "Well, I wanted you to have a betrothal ring."

Her eyes rounded. "Betrothal," she repeated in a whisper, obviously having trouble sorting what he intended.

He kissed her. "I secured a special license when we were in Doctors' Commons yesterday. If you'd like, we can wed Monday."

"Monday?" she repeated, incredulous. "That's Christmas Eve."

"Indeed. I can think of no better Christmas present than to find you next to me when I wake up that day."

"You wish to wed me?" she asked in a whisper. Here she had been thinking he meant only to have her warm his bed on occasion.

He hadn't exactly proposed marriage.

He blinked. "Well, yes. Why are you looking at me as if I'm a candidate for Bedlam?"

She scoffed, scooting away from him so she could look at him directly. "Mayhap because you are?"

He furrowed a brow. "I assure you, I've never been more sane in all my life," he claimed. "And if you dare claim you're still in mourning—"

"I wouldn't. I am not," she interrupted, remembering all too quickly what they had discovered in the will the day before.

"Then... why are you so surprised?" he asked, his expression suggesting he was hurt by her reaction.

Elaine inhaled as if to speak and found she didn't have an appropriate response. She swallowed. "Because these sorts of things don't happen to me?" she guessed.

Edward chuckled. "I've been without a marchioness for far too long," he murmured. "Without a *wife* for far too long. Yesterday's sojourn with you reminded me of what I've been missing."

Staring at him for a time, Elaine's gaze traveled down his naked body, her own reacting in a most pleasant manner, as if it remembered all too well what he had done to her in the middle of the night.

As if his cock knew of her attentions, it stiffened before her eyes. She inhaled softly and turned her gaze back on his face. "Why me?" she asked.

His own gaze darted to his cock, as if his erection was answer enough. At her slight scoff, he sighed and lay back in the pillows. "Someone needs to spoil you," he said. "I wish to be that someone."

"I hardly think that's grounds for wishing to marry someone."

He considered her response for a moment before he said, "I want you to be Lady Catherine's grandmother, and I rather think she does, too."

Elaine scoffed, this time more loudly. "How can you know such a thing?"

It was his turn to scoff. "She ran to *you*," he replied. "She's never met you before, and yet she somehow knew *you* would be the one to say the right thing. Trust you enough that she could fall asleep in your arms."

Her heart clenching at the reminder of carrying the small girl to the nursery in Delton House, Elaine sighed. "All right." She regarded him a moment, secretly heartened at how he appeared so proud of himself. "Is there any other reason?"

He sighed. "Oh, all right. Since I fired my man of business, I am in need of someone to see to my ledgers," he admitted.

She grinned. "You could have started with that," she teased.

Pulling her so she ended up straddled atop him, he growled, "You minx."

## CHAPTER 14
## CHRISTMAS EVE

*wo days later*
"I cannot understand why, but I am nervous," Edward muttered as he stood next to Elaine. They were in St. Paul's church, waiting for the priest to begin their wedding ceremony. Both her sons, Graham and Gabriel, were there, too, standing off to one side. At any moment, Edward's son, John, would be joining them.

"As am I." Elaine grinned as she glanced over at him, remembering all too well what he had looked like earlier that morning, naked and surrounded by pink. Unlike the morning before, they'd been forced to leave the comfortable bed to see to that day's wedding.

The two had departed the Soho Club in his town coach, and Edward had left her at Montaine House to change clothes while he went on to Delton House to do the same. Two hours later, with the clock threatening half-past-eleven in the morning, the two had entered St. Paul's breathless and laughing.

Edward looked the part of his title on this morning. Besides his bright white shirt and cravat, he was wearing a dark navy topcoat and gray pantaloons. His waistcoat, cut from silver silk, was embellished with colorful embroidery of a rather elaborate design featuring birds and butterflies. His short top hat was in the care of one of her sons.

He hadn't known Elaine would be wearing a gown of cobalt blue with a silver sarcenet overdress, so the two had stared at one another a moment when he came to collect her at Montaine House. "Great minds," Edward had announced before he leaned down and kissed her—right in front of Graham and the butler. Gabriel, who had returned from university only the Saturday before, hadn't yet appeared from his bedchamber.

Elaine had come down the stairs to discover her oldest son shaking the marquess' hand. Overhearing Graham's comment, "I had no idea my mother was even being court-ed," she struggled to keep a straight face as she joined them in the hall.

"I hardly see you these days," she remarked as she noted that Graham had dressed especially fine for the ceremony. "And besides, it was Delton's idea that we wed before Christmas." She had given Edward a prim grin. "I cannot think of a better present to find on Christmas morn than you."

About to accuse her of stealing his line, Edward was forced to step aside when several footmen appeared from the vestibule, their arms laden with pine boughs. The scent of evergreen trees immediately filled the hall.

"Where would you like them, my lady?" the first footman had asked from behind the branches he held.

Elaine glanced over at Graham. "It's your decision, darling. This is your house now."

His jaw dropping, Graham seemed at a loss until the housekeeper appeared from the back of the house. "Oh, finally," she had said with a huge grin. "Follow me. We'll have this house decorated in no time."

Obviously relieved at not having to direct the servants in the hanging of the greens, Graham had called up to his brother, urging him to hurry his descent down the stairs. "What kind of witnesses will we be if we miss our mother's wedding?"

Gabriel bowed before the marquess as Elaine made the introductions. "It's an honor to meet you, my lord," Gabriel had said, not used to having to look up at another person given his height. "I know your son from school. He's older, but—"

"Oh, dear," Edward deadpanned before a smile split his face. "Did you bring him home with you?"

Gabriel had given a start. "He left about the same time as I did, so he should have reached London Saturday evening."

Edward continued to grin. "My butler assured me he arrived in one piece." He had turned to Elaine and added, "I'm quite sure Lady Catherine was up well past her bedtime."

"Will I meet John today?" Elaine asked.

Nodding, Edward said, "With any luck, at the church. He was dressing when I left Delton House."

John made it in time, managing to look rather dapper in his formal attire despite the short notice. "You must be the woman Cathy was babbling about last night," he said after Edward had introduced him to Elaine. "She thinks the world of you."

The odd sensation Elaine had experienced two days ago once again had her inhaling softly. "I assure you, sir, the feeling is mutual," she had replied. She had nearly forgotten she would be a grandmother in only a few moments' time.

. . .

*A*s flutterbies danced about in her stomach, Elaine allowed Edward to lead her to where the priest was waiting for them. Words were spoken, vows were exchanged, and another ring—this one a gold band—appeared and was slid onto the fourth finger of her left hand.

"Three days," she whispered after the priest had pronounced them married.

"What happens in three days?" Edward asked after he kissed her.

Elaine smiled and then tittered. "Our entire courtship," she replied.

Edward's eyes darkened. "We'll have your house all to ourselves on Boxing Day," he said, knowing the servants would be visiting their families. He had taken Elaine to the dower house the day before, enjoying her look of surprise when she realized it was only a few doors down from his townhouse in South Audley Street. "And by then, the bed will have been delivered."

Her eyes rounding, Elaine asked, "What bed?"

Edward chuckled. "The one from the Pink Room. It took some doing and a good deal of blunt, but I was finally able to talk Mrs. Skarsgard into selling it to me."

Elaine gasped. "For the mistress suite?"

Scoffing, Edward said, "For the master suite, my sweeting. I wanted to be sure you'll be joining me in my bed every night."

Blushing a bright pink, Elaine whispered, "I would join you every night even if there wasn't a bed at all."

Edward seemed to consider her response a moment before he nodded. "I could probably cancel the transaction," he suggested, feigning indecision.

"You'll do no such thing," she replied, grinning when he guffawed. "Come. Let's go have breakfast," she urged, remembering the Delton House cook was planning the meal for their small wedding party.

"The pine boughs will have been delivered by now," Edward said as they made their way out of the church. Their sons followed, seeing to their own introductions and sharing their surprise at learning they were to gain a parent that day.

"After breakfast, we can do a proper hanging of the greens," Elaine said as she allowed Edward to help her into the carriage that would take them to Delton House. "And I can do the ribbons."

"After which we can engage in some improper behavior," he said, waggling his brows as he settled next to her.

Elaine blushed but waggled her own brows. "I'll be sure to save a length of red ribbon to decorate you."

It was Edward's turn to blush.

# AUTHOR NOTES

### *Inheritance in the 1800s*

To ensure one's descendants received what was incurred, a system known as *primogeniture* was put in place. Primogeniture meant that all the land in each generation's possession was left to the eldest son in the family rather than being divided equally among off the offspring.

In the case of dukedoms, marquessates, earldoms and viscountcies, the land and sometimes the properties were *entailed*, which meant they couldn't be sold off or inherited by anyone other than the next in line for the title.

*Unentailed* properties could be inherited, however, which meant they could be sold off or gambled away.

**Your Invitation!**

Do you crave historical romance filled with passion and red hot chemistry?

Come join me and my author friends in the Facebook group, Historical Harlots, for exclusive giveaways, chats with amazing HistRom authors, raunchy shenanigans, and more! https://www.facebook.com/groups/2102138599813601

# ABOUT THE AUTHOR

A self-described nerd and student of history, Linda Rae spent many years as a published technical writer specializing in 3D graphics workstations, software and 3D animation (her movie credits include SHREK and SHREK 2). Getting lost in the rabbit holes of research has resulted in historical romances set in the Regency-era as well as Ancient Greece.

A fan of action-adventure movies, she can frequently be found at the local cinema. Although she no longer has any tropical fish, she follows the San Jose Sharks and makes her home in Cody, Wyoming.

*For more information:*
www.lindaraesande.com
*Sign up for Linda Rae's newsletter:*
Regency Romance with a Twist
*Follow Linda Rae's blog:*
Regency Romance with a Twist

www.ingramcontent.com/pod-product-compliance
Lightning Source LLC
Chambersburg PA
CBHW031256210726
48287CB00003B/1053